Soft L… os

Kim Step… son

Happy ~~Running~~ Reading

Kim

Running for the Romance

Author's Note

The characters, setting and author of *Soft Landings* are British, so the book is written in British English.

Though not jargon heavy, you may come across some unfamiliar words related to running. A handy glossary of running terminology is provided at the back of the book for reference.

Soft Landings is a romantic comedy though it does contain themes that may be troubling to some readers including reference to homophobia and minor sport-related injury.

ISBN Paperback: 978-1-0684398-2-7

Cover Design: 100Covers

Interior Formatting: Kim Stephenson

For anyone with a big change ahead, may your landing be soft.

Contents

About the author

soft landing (n.) In biomechanics and running: a landing technique involving increased flexion at the ankle, knee, and hip joints to reduce ground reaction forces, thereby minimising injury risk by absorbing impact more effectively.

adapted from: Davis, I. S., Bowser, B. J., & Mullineaux, D. R. (2014).

Chapter 1

Sebastien

8 WEEKS TO THE SCOTLAND 100

The weird thing about beginnings is that they often disguise themselves as endings. Sebastien snorted at the obnoxiously erudite thought that floated through his mind as he loaded the last of his luggage into his dad's boot for the drive back to London. Maybe those were the kinds of thoughts you ended up with when you dated someone reading for an English degree. He should've known better. Either that or he'd just been in Oxford too long. Now, though, after five years in the city of dreaming spires, he was leaving it all behind to return to his childhood home in London. And he did mean leaving it all behind. A strangely numb feeling took over as he thought back to the conversation he'd had with his boyfriend—ex-boyfriend now—the night before.

It had been a completely mutual decision, and that was probably the worst thing about it. Neither of them was at fault; they were just on very different paths, and it didn't make sense to carry on. It had never been love, what they had. Sebastien knew it, Darius knew it, so it made sense to part ways as they finished uni and moved on with their lives.

It wasn't so much the breakup with Darius that smarted, but the knowledge that the "different path" Darius was on was one Sebastien himself had expected to be on. He'd trained just as hard for just as long, but with one injury too many, Seb knew his future as a professional athlete was over before it had even truly started.

That was the real reason he'd known he needed to end things; he couldn't imagine what it would have been like to be there, watching his partner achieve all the things he'd dreamed of while he struggled to find his footing in a new career. A clean break was needed. So that was what they'd given each other.

It wasn't like Sebastien was running home with his tail between his legs—he had a plan and knew he'd be fine. He was a fully qualified physiotherapist now, having finished his master's at a lesser-known university than the hallowed halls of his bachelor's degree and gained a more practical qualification.

Unlike many of his course-mates, who were giving themselves on last summer off before entering the world of work, he had a job at a major clinic chain as a junior physio that would start next week. It wasn't the dream, but at least this time he'd be sticking closer to home.

Being back in London also meant he'd be able to save a fortune in rent by living with his parents. It wasn't always the done thing in other parts of the country, but living with your parents in London wasn't unusual for young people trying to get a foot on the career ladder these days, and he wasn't going to pass up the opportunity to save a bit of money.

Sebastien's dad surveyed his four suitcases with the judgemental eyes of someone who had never had to suffer through carting equipment around, trying to build up his experience with all the university sports teams he could. Though his didn't comment as he shoved the bags into the boot and back seat of his car, Sebastien could practically hear his thoughts.

"Shut it," Sebastien said.

His dad laughed. "I didn't say anything."

They settled in for the drive, and it was silent apart from BBC Radio 4 droning on in the background.

"So, will Darius be joining us over the summer?" his dad asked, prompting a wince from Sebastien.

"Unlikely, seeing as we've broken up."

His dad let out a sigh. "But you were so good together. He's so driven, and it's good for you to have someone like that around."

"Dad, can we not? It's still pretty fresh."

To his credit, his dad did turn his attention back to the road and the radio for the next fifteen minutes or so, giving Sebastien a chance to relax into his seat and process.

"Did you know Nathan got back last week? Siobhan and Carl are happy to have him back in the country."

Sebastien nodded. He did know.

"You two still talk then? You used to have such a crush on him."

Flushing, Sebastien turned to look out the window. It was a universal truth that nothing ever quite measured up to the feeling of your first love, but for Sebastien, that first love had been both all-encompassing and entirely one-sided. Nathan had been a year above him at school, and from the moment his family had moved in next door, he'd become Sebastien's whole world. He'd definitely only seen him as a friend though, and they'd drifted apart a bit with the distance.

God, at first, he'd been no more than an annoyance to Nathan, he was sure. Just the younger kid who had hero-worshipped him.

Nathan had been a star athlete at their school, and the star of Seb's earliest fantasies. With his wavy blonde hair and muscular build, Seb had certainly not been the only one at their school half in love with him back then. Nathan had also been the initial inspiration for Sebastien taking up running, having let him jog with him on Saturday mornings when he did his long runs. Sebastien had looked forward to those all week, planning out conversation points so he could look cool in front of the older boy.

Running together had eventually turned into a genuine friendship that had carried on until Nathan had gone to America on a scholarship for his athletics prowess, and Sebastien had spent his final year of high school determined to move on from the straight, older boy who would never see him as more than a friend. They'd kept in touch, though, their friendship firm enough by then to hold up despite the distance. Much to his chagrin, even with years and distance between them, Sebastien still judged every potential partner against the impossible standard Nathan had set.

As his parents' house in Islington came into view, something settled in Sebastien's chest, leaving him more at ease than he had been in weeks. It was good to be back. His dad navigated down the leafy street that felt so far removed from the hustle and bustle of Central London, despite being just a handful of tube stops from the busy tourist hub of Trafalgar Square. His parents still lived in the four-bedroom terraced house he'd grown up in, and Sebastien knew living with them again was going to be a massive adjustment.

The door to the house was flung open, and his mother rushed out before he even had a chance to get out of the still-running car. His dad killed the engine as she darted forwards to engulf Sebastien in a hug as he clambered out.

"Would you look at that, Marie? Our little boy, home at last," his dad said.

Sebastien's mum smiled indulgently. The two of them couldn't have been more different. His mother, Marie, was a tall, willowy French woman. She was a partner in a global law firm and had taken up ultramarathon running in her fifties. Now, at fifty-five, she was a well-known figure in the ultra community, with a large collection of belt buckles from hundred-mile-plus races. She was forever trying to get Sebastien to give a fifty miler a try. He wasn't having it, but he had agreed to crew for her and pace a couple of legs of her next race—a hundred-mile effort in Scotland that was just a couple months away. Privately, Seb thought his mum may have a screw loose.

His father, on the other hand, was a stout Scottish man with a thick, greying beard. The tiny spectacles he always had perched on his nose added the finishing touch to his mad professor look. Technically, he could retire from his job as a professor of graphic design at Central Saint Martins, but Sebastien didn't think that day would ever come. His dad *loved* his job in a way so few people truly do. Growing up, it had given him hope that he'd find the one thing that brought joy into his life, instead of just paying the bills. He hoped physio would be that for him. Once upon a time, he'd truly believed athletics would be.

"Sebastien, how could you possibly have accumulated this much stuff? You left with one suitcase."

Sebastien shrugged off his mum's commentary. It wasn't just his equipment. Darius had bought him a lot of things over the last year, probably to make up for not being willing to be seen with him in public.

"Well, let's get you settled inside." His mum grabbed a couple of bags and made for the door. Sebastien picked up the last of his suitcases and slung his backpack over his shoulder, making his way inside.

Chapter 2
Nathan

8 WEEKS TO THE SCOTLAND 100

The window of Nathan's childhood bedroom looked right out onto the quiet street below, so it had been impossible to miss the rumbling black car pulling up next door; the Murphys weren't quiet about anything they did, and their car was no exception. For Nathan, it had been even more impossible to miss the attractive man who'd stepped out, only to be immediately engulfed in a tight embrace by Marie.

Sebastien was back.

Nathan absentmindedly scratched behind the ears of his rescue greyhound, Mabel, as she sprawled next to him on the window seat. He watched Sebastien interact with his parents, an easy smile stretching across his face as he unloaded suitcase after suitcase from the car.

Sebastien looked bloody good.

His mahogany hair was a riot of curls. A couple of rogue ringlets fell just around his ears, and his glasses did little to hide the bright green of his eyes, even from a distance. Nathan couldn't help but notice how fit he was too, his broad shoulders and trim waist easily discernible under the tight-fitting blue Henley he wore.

He knew his own mum would want to head over there as soon as possible to welcome Sebastien home, but being surrounded by their parents, with his life in a mess wasn't quite the scenario Nathan had hoped for in terms of a reunion with the younger boy who'd held his attention all through school.

Sebastien and Nathan had been close for as long as he could remember, and for a while, he'd thought maybe... But he'd been warned off, and then Seb had ended up in a relationship with Nathan's little sister, Angela. Nathan had started to put distance between them then, because seeing them together had made his heart feel like it had been carved out of his chest. As if there wasn't already enough lingering jealousy and resentment between him and Ang.

Sebastien hadn't let that distance grow, though, even when they'd been apart. He'd always prioritised Nathan, making him feel like the worst friend in the world for letting his wildly inconvenient feelings come between them. Seb and Ang hadn't lasted long, and Nathan knew Sebastien had been seeing a man at Oxford, but he hadn't been able to get much information about him, and honestly, he'd never pushed, not really wanting to hear about Sebastien being happy in a relationship with someone who wasn't him.

He'd been a shit friend, and he was well aware of it.

Being jobless, single, and moving back in with his mum at age twenty-five was bad enough. He didn't need to twist the knife by having Sebastien see how far he'd fallen.

They were friends now, though, and no matter how much Nathan longed for more, he wouldn't give that friendship up for anything. He was going to do better.

Sebastien had been his lifeline when he'd first realised he wasn't going to go all the way in athletics, or track, as he'd started to refer to the sport after his first couple of years in America. Sebastien had talked him off the ledge, almost literally, convincing him to finish his degree even when it looked like his poor performance might cost him his scholarship.

In the end, he'd managed to hang on to it until the end of his five-year eligibility and finish out his degree. Less than a year later, though, he'd flown home with his tail between his legs, no job offers, and no sponsorships.

At least he'd been able to bring Mabs with him.

When, inevitably, his mum shouted up the stairs that she was heading next door, he shouted right back down that he couldn't join, feigning pain in his shoulder. Well, he wasn't completely feigning it. The pain in his shoulder was a constant these days, but it wasn't so debilitating that he couldn't have popped next door for a cuppa.

After a couple of hours of lazing around his room feeling sorry for himself, he grabbed Mabel's lead and made for the door. Mabel waited obediently as he clipped the lead to her collar, then headed out with him into the fading evening light. They hadn't made it more than five steps when the door of the house next door swung open and the very man he had been trying to avoid stepped out.

"Nathaniel Elias Steele. What a sight for sore eyes you are." Sebastien's face was alight with playfulness as he approached. "And is this Mabel? Oh, aren't you a sweet girl?" He crouched to stroke Mabel's ears, and she immediately leaned into his warmth.

An absolute sucker for attention, that one.

Nathan openly stared at Sebastien as he snuggled up to the dog. He looked even better up close. Photos and video calls truly didn't do him justice. "Bloody good to see you, mate."

Sebastien didn't seem to notice Nathan's ogling, his attention still fully focused on Mabel. "Mind if I join you two? I've got to get away from the inquisition for a bit."

"They going hard on you?" Nathan asked.

Sebastien sighed, running a hand through his mahogany hair. "Mum and Dad aren't thrilled about my breakup. They're obsessed with him, I swear."

"How recent?"

"Last night."

Nathan let out a low whistle. "Shit. I'm sorry."

Sebastien shrugged. "It's not a big deal. We're just better as friends. Don't want the same things, you know?"

"Let me guess, Keith talked about him all the way home?"

"Alternated between that, how to recover my athletics career, and ranting at the radio."

"Radio 4?"

"Is there another station?"

Nathan laughed. "Saw you arrive. Looked like you brought all of Oxford back with you."

Sebastien shot him a quizzical look. "You saw me arrive and didn't come and say hello?" It was hard to tell whether the hurt on his face was genuine or a wind-up. "Harsh, Nate. I thought we were friends."

"It wasn't that," Nathan insisted. "I wanted to, I was just... Well, I wanted a chance to make the right kind of impression."

"Oh? And what kind of impression would that be?"

Nathan stuttered out a breath. There was something in Sebastien's tone that almost sounded heated. He must have been imagining it, though. Must have been hearing what he wanted to rather than what was really there.

"I'm just giving you shit." Sebastien laughed. "You've been in America too long; can't keep up with the bants anymore."

"Please tell me you did not just say bants."

"I know. I regretted it the second it left my mouth."

They walked in silence for a few minutes. The awkwardness subsided as they strolled slowly through the neighbourhood they both knew so well, Mabel loping along beside them.

"I was kind of avoiding you, though."

"Why?" Sebastien asked.

"You know, back in school I was, like, the cool athlete. Felt like maybe you looked up to me then. Didn't want you to see what a mess my life turned out to be."

"Please, you were never that cool. And you seem to be doing fine from where I'm standing."

Nathan scoffed as he tugged Mabel along towards the park. "I barely made it through college, ended my athletics career prematurely, and got dumped. Excuse me if it's not looking all that impressive from my perspective."

"All I'm hearing is that you're a fit single guy with a degree who makes good financial decisions." Sebastien smiled easily.

All Nathan heard was that Sebastien thought he was fit.

He was probably just humouring him, though, trying to big him up. He was nice like that, always trying to help people. Sebastien had everything together. He could probably tell how desperate Nathan was for his approval. He rolled his shoulder slightly, trying to shake off the ache that always came when he tensed up.

"Shoulder bothering you?"

Nathan sighed. "Injured it back in January and it hasn't quite healed right."

"Let me take a look?"

Blinking dumbly at Sebastien, Nathan nodded his assent, not even entirely certain what it was he was agreeing to. Then Sebastien's hands were on his shoulders, gently kneading the muscle. His fingers made Nathan let out a sigh of relief, almost melting into a puddle of goo under his ministrations until he hit that one spot that made pain fire through his nerve endings like he'd been electrocuted.

"Ah-hah! There it is." Sebastien dug his fingers in again, torturing Nathan.

Maybe this was retribution for leaving all those years ago. It certainly felt like revenge of some kind.

"Your shoulder is all kinds of fucked up. I've got some of my equipment in the house. If you want, I can help you treat that, get you back on your feet—or shoulder, as it were—a bit faster."

"Are you planning to torture me even more?"

"Only if you want me to." The flirtatious effect was slightly ruined by how red Sebastien turned before he coughed and corrected himself. "I mean, it'll hurt at first, but it will start to improve, you just had a bunch of muscles and nerves all crunched up together there."

"Right, I sort of forgot you studied physio."

"I'm fully trained and qualified; starting my first grown-up job in a week," Sebastien reminded him.

Nathan smiled at him. Of course Sebastien was headed straight into a job—he'd done everything exactly according to plan to get where he wanted to. Nathan, on the other hand, was just floating around, hoping something would fall into his lap. "Yeah, you always were a little nerd. Don't know how it slipped my mind."

"You seriously forgot? You just let random people manhandle you in the street, then?" Sebastien joked.

"You're hardly a random person, Sebastien."

"Yeah?" Sebastien asked softly.

"I mean, I've known you since you were seven and once saw you eat a worm you dug out of the dirt in the front garden."

"It was one time! And you dared me to!"

"Still gross."

Sebastien shuddered involuntarily. The conversation died down as they continued the slow stroll towards the park, Mabel a steady presence, her lead slack.

When they arrived, Nathan unclipped her lead and pulled a tennis ball out of his coat pocket.

"Aren't you worried she'll run off?"

Nathan laughed. "This old girl? Nah. She's got a good sprint in her, but she'd lie down for a nap after about a minute even if she did bolt."

Mabel was the best thing he'd got out of his last relationship. He'd been with Holly for two years, and he'd really tried with her, but as it had become clear Nathan wouldn't be heading for the Olympics and a lucrative sponsorship contract after college, things had started to fall apart. They'd adopted Mabel just a few months after they'd first moved in together, but she'd always been more Nathan's dog than Holly's. Maybe he felt a strange sort of kinship with her; she was a washed-up sprinter too.

He snorted at the thought.

"What's so funny?"

"Just mentally comparing myself to a retired racing dog."

Sebastien grinned. "I can see it. It's in the nose."

Nathan shoved his shoulder lightly, and they chatted about everything and nothing as Nathan tossed the ball for Mabel. When she'd clearly had enough and come back to lie down at his feet, he settled on the grass beside her, and Sebastien did the same.

"You weren't kidding about the laziness then?"

Mabel rolled over onto her back in response. Sebastien took the hint and rubbed her belly as they continued to chat.

"So, what's your plan then?" Sebastien asked. "Back for good?"

Nathan paused. It had been eating at him from the moment he stepped through his parents' front door, the fact that he didn't actually have much of a plan at all. "I'm looking for work, so I'll just go wherever I find it, really. Not sure about sticking around here though. Living with the parents isn't exactly my long-term dream."

Sebastien hummed thoughtfully but didn't comment. Something about his posture changed, though, almost like he'd deflated. Moments later though, he was on his feet, joking with Nathan again about needing to get back before curfew.

The short walk back left them standing in front of the houses, neither quite willing to part to go inside.

"Are you still training, despite the—" Sebastien made a gesture towards Nate's shoulder, attempting to dispel the weird tension that had fallen over them.

"Thought about it," Nathan replied. "I probably should start soon before I lose all my fitness."

"We could run together. I mean, if you want to. I'm actually going to be pacing Mum in a race in a couple months, could be fun if you wanted to join. We could travel up together. It'd be like a camping trip but with running. I mean, I get it if you don't want to though. I know pacing isn't the same, but it's usually pretty fun and—god, I'm rambling. I'll stop."

"You're fine. And yeah, I'd love to join you, sounds fun."

Seb beamed at him, and Nathan wasn't sure how he'd survived five years without seeing that grin in person.

Nathan took Mabel inside and got her settled for the night before retiring to his room, determined not to spend the night dreaming about the boy next door.

Chapter 3
Sebastien

8 WEEKS TO THE SCOTLAND 100

After breakfast with his parents, during which his mother enthusiastically thanked him for roping in another crew member with such exuberance that he felt nervous for Nathan, Sebastien was feeling unusually energised but with very little to actually do. With his first proper job starting in a week and uni really and truly behind him, his free time was completely free, perhaps for the first time. He'd never been good at sitting idle, though, always wanting something to occupy his time. Rest felt like he was being unproductive, lazy even. It was one of the things he'd had in common with Darius.

As Sebastien scrolled idly on his phone, one of Darius's recent photos popped up on his screen: a simple post-run snap of his smartwatch with his trainers in the background. The only emotion it sparked in Sebastien was a sliver of humour at the thought that someone was probably on Darius to grow his social media presence. There wasn't a chance in hell he'd have posted anything otherwise.

He was surprised that his heart didn't lurch. As much as it had been mutual, breakups were meant to hurt. He didn't think he should be over it yet. God knew it had taken him months to pull himself together after breaking up with Angie. Maybe it was because he'd been younger then. Or maybe it was because the breakup with

Angie had come with a healthy side of fear that he'd lose Nathan in the deal.

Think of the devil and all that... The buzzer rang, and Sebastien leapt to answer it before his dad could get there. Though his mum spent most days in her Central London office, his dad had thoroughly embraced working from home and rarely went in unless he was lecturing or had office hours, which were becoming less and less frequent; his interests turning much more towards research in recent years.

Nathan was at the door with a sheepish grin on his face.

"Sorry. I know you're probably busy, but I thought I'd see if you wanted to go on a run with me, maybe help me ease back into it?"

"You're fine, come in." As if Sebastien wouldn't drop any plans he did have to spend time with Nathan. Shaking the thought from his mind, he beckoned Nathan into the house. "You want a cuppa or anything first?" he asked, already putting the kettle on to boil before Nathan's affirmative. He moved with practiced ease, preparing Nathan's tea the way he'd done a thousand times before in this very kitchen.

"How are you doing?" Sebastien asked. "And more importantly, how's my best girl?"

"Angie?" Nathan asked, a confused and maybe even slightly hurt tone in his voice.

"I meant Mabel, but sure, we can go there if you want."

The tension drained from Nathan's body. "Mabel's good. She'll spend the day in Dad's office trying to mooch off him and cleaning up any biscuit crumbs he drops on the floor."

Sebastien noticed the distinct avoidance of talk of his sister Angie, but didn't call him out on it. He was curious—the two of them had been thick as thieves when they were kids—but Ang wasn't exactly a topic Sebastien was dying to explore.

At sixteen, Sebastien had embarked on his very ill-fated attempt at dating Angie. It was his last-ditch effort to prove he could like girls, but it had been very apparent to everyone involved that he was carrying a torch for her brother, one that had already proven to be unreciprocated. Angie had known, Sebastien had known, but breaking up with her had still been one of the hardest things he'd ever done. He felt a lot of guilt over that time of his life, even now. It wasn't until he got to university and made queer friends that he really realised what he'd been doing, and how much energy he'd been putting into trying to be someone he wasn't.

Sebastien thought he'd grown. He was a man of the world now, but apparently, he couldn't move past his first schoolboy crush.

"So, start easy today? Slow 5k, just to ease back in?" Sebastien suggested tentatively.

Nathan nodded. "Sounds good, I've done nothing at all for weeks, so don't laugh when I barely make it past the end of the road."

"I would never," Sebastien gasped dramatically.

"Sure you wouldn't, you little shithead."

"God, can really feel the love here. So nice to be on the same continent again."

Nathan bumped his shoulder as he hopped down from the stool, looking ready to hit the pavement, and Sebastien couldn't hold back his grin.

"Someone's keen. At least let me change first." He gestured to the pyjama bottoms he was wearing.

Nathan smiled sheepishly. "I'll just wait here for you, then?"

"You can come up if you like." Sebastien said it almost flirtatiously. The proximity to Nathan was clearly short-circuiting the rational pathways in his brain, but the widening of Nathan's eyes had him backtracking immediately. "I'm joking, mate. Wait here. Obviously."

The streets of Islington unfolded before them as they left the house and jogged slowly towards the green.

"Look at you go. Already made it past the end of the road," Sebastien said.

Nathan huffed out a laugh. "Only 'cause you're going easy on me."

"Well, I wouldn't want to break you on your first day. Fragile sprinter and all. How will I convince you to run an ultra of your own if I scare you off now?"

Nathan scrunched up his nose. "The idea of running more than a marathon is utterly horrifying. I just don't see the reason for it. I'm stressed enough about getting through this 5k with you."

"Mum would argue it's barely even a run if it's under fifty."

Nathan shuddered. "No, thank you. I think I'll stick to the eight hundred metres. I get the feeling pacing Marie is already going to push my limits."

Sebastien laughed. He didn't disagree exactly, but as a distance runner it was his sworn duty to take the piss out of sprinters at every possible opportunity. "Yeah, you're right. You probably couldn't handle it."

"Excuse you. I'm a two-time NCAA eight hundred metre champion. I can handle it."

"It gets harder with age, though, and you're basically retired."

"Let's find one, right now. Find me an ultra. I'm going to out-ultra your arse and I will be laughing at you from the finish line."

"Competitive much?" Seb arched a brow.

Nathan flushed, obviously embarrassed, though Sebastien wasn't sure why. Nathan had been hyper-competitive for as long as he'd known him. About everything.

If Sebastien had been in the mood for analysing himself, he might have noted that his attraction to Darius had initially been because of that competitiveness he'd seen as reminiscent of Nathan.

"Sorry," Nathan replied after a beat.

Sebastien laughed. "It's okay, I know you can't help it. It's the curse of all short-distance guys—more ego than grit."

"I'll show you grit," Nathan grunted.

Sebastien knew Nathan well enough that what happened next shouldn't have been a surprise. He knew Nathan was competitive, that he always felt he had something to prove; there was nothing he could do to stop him really. Nathan pumped his arms harder to pick up speed, and seconds later, a cry tore through the air. Sebastien caught up to Nathan, who had stopped dead, gripping his shoulder with a look of anguish on his face.

"Are you okay?" Sebastien asked. It was a stupid question. Of course he wasn't okay. He was in pain.

"I'll be fine." Nathan groaned. "Hurts like hell, but mostly I just feel like an idiot."

"Come on, let's walk back and I'll take a proper look at it. I don't want you coming to Scotland if it's going to make your injury worse."

"I want to train with you, though. You'll start work next week, and you'll be training—we'll never see each other if I can't even run with you."

"Nate, we live next door to each other. We'll hang out. I promise," Sebastien said. He'd make time for Nathan no matter what. "Now, let's go. I want to see what's going on with that shoulder."

Sebastien led Nathan into the house. A frisson of excitement ran through him at the idea of getting his hands on Nathan. Shaking the wildly unprofessional thought from his mind, he beckoned for Nathan to follow him up to his room.

Sebastien grimaced at the sight of his suitcases shoved up against a wall, barely unpacked. The room was full of old books and boxes of his trophies and medals. Looking at those felt like another life.

Nathan sat on the edge of Sebastien's bed, shucking his shirt with no preamble to give Sebastien a completely uninhibited view of the planes of hard muscle under his soft tan skin. His mouth went dry. Nathan had certainly not got worse with age.

"So, looks like I get to be your first patient. You looking forward to starting for real next week?"

Sebastien shook himself out of the staring competition he'd been having with Nathan's abs. "I guess. I can't quite shake the feeling that I should be doing something more impactful with my degree or, I don't know, staying more connected to athletics," he said as he examined the shoulder that was giving Nathan so much grief, his fingers ghosting over the skin and dipping into the crevices to get a feel for the knots and tension in the muscle.

"I get that. I'd love to stay close to the sport too, but right now I'll take whatever I can get."

"So, tell me about your injury." He tried to get them back on track, and he was curious; Nathan hadn't mentioned an injury when they'd spoken recently. But then, he hadn't mentioned moving back home with his parents or a breakup either, so maybe they'd drifted apart even more than Sebastien had realised.

"So, obviously, you know my running career didn't exactly end in a blaze of glory," Nathan said.

"Happens to the best of us."

"Sorry. I know that must be pretty fresh for you." Nathan winced. "I don't know how you're feeling about it or what happened."

"You're fine, Nate. I just... Well, I've had one too many injuries, you know? And I'd like to be able to walk in my seventies. I don't want to give it up completely, but I needed to get some space from it all when I realised I wasn't going to go the distance, so to speak."

"Is that what happened with your boyfriend? He's gone pro, you said?"

Sebastien sighed and nodded. "Part of it, for sure." That pretty much hit the nail on the head, actually.

"Well, you've got a way healthier attitude about it than I had. Losing running felt like...like carving out a piece of myself and leaving it behind." Sebastien understood that on some level, but he'd always known that the likelihood of succeeding in sports was low, and his back-up plan was solid. He'd always been practical like that.

Sebastien pushed down on a muscle in Nathan's shoulder and held until he felt it shift and release.

Nate let out a sigh.

"So how did you do this? You said it's been a while?"

Nathan shifted on the table. "It's stupid."

"I doubt that."

Nate arched a brow in a challenging manner. "My ex-girlfriend. When I announced I was retiring from running after college, she wasn't happy about it. We went on this ski trip, a sort of last-ditch attempt to save our relationship, really, and a bunch of her friends were there. There was this guy, real cool fucker, professional golfer, great skier, constantly trying to chat her up even right in front of me."

Nathan looked uncomfortable talking about this, like maybe this was the first time he'd admitted it to anyone.

"Anyway, I got jealous, and when I get jealous, I get competitive."

Sebastien made a strangled noise in the back of his throat as he tried to hold back a laugh. Nathan had always been like that.

"Went up a double black with them that I was wildly unqualified to attempt and fell badly on the moguls. Had to get taken down on a snowmobile and everything. Had a massive blow-up with Holly over it and flew home by myself with my arm in a sling."

"You never mentioned any of this," Sebastien said.

"Yeah, well. Bit embarrassing, innit? It's fine. It was nearly six months ago now, and I'm over it. I got to keep Mabel in the deal."

"You definitely won that one then." Sebastien grinned.

"Yeah, I thought the shoulder would feel better by now, but apparently it's not going to sort itself out."

Sebastien hummed in consideration. He pressed his fingers into a couple more places on Nate's shoulder as he considered the way the muscles felt beneath. Then he moved to the opposite side and slid his hands over Nate's ribcage.

"Erm, what's happening right now?"

"Your initial injury did heal, but the muscles are knotted up so bad it probably doesn't feel much better."

"That's why you're tracing every inch of my skin?"

"It's all connected." Sebastien gestured for Nathan to sit up and lean forward. He traced a line down his back, around to his ribs. "Strain here can be caused by overcompensating here," he explained.

"Ah. Thought maybe you just wanted to get your hands on me."

"And if I did?" Sebastien felt like his mouth had fully disconnected from his brain. Nate had never shown even an inkling of interest in men, much less in Sebastien.

"Then that would be very okay with me," Nathan replied.

Sebastien nearly choked as he spluttered, trying to think of a response. His hands stilled, and he pulled them back as if he'd been burned. "Don't joke about that, Nate. It isn't fair."

Nathan looked contrite. So Sebastien had got it right—just banter gone one step too far, not genuine interest. He scolded himself for how disappointed he was about that. The last thing he needed right now was to go diving head first into a new relationship. He'd been single for all of two days.

It was Nate, though. They may have known each other for years, but they'd never touched each other, not like that. Sure, it was all under the guise of getting Nathan to a relatively pain-free existence, as if that was even possible for runners, but the thought of tracing his warm skin would have kept Sebastien going for weeks. Nate clearly saw him as a joke, though, the silly boy next door with a crush on his straight neighbour. Christ, he was such a bloody cliché.

Sebastien threw Nathan his shirt as he tidied up. It wouldn't be worth risking their friendship anyway, not when he'd just got Nate back in his life. Nate was watching him, clearly uncomfortable now, and he worried he'd overreacted to a simple, playful comment.

Chapter 4
Nathan

7 WEEKS TO THE SCOTLAND 100

Nathan spent the entire week replaying his own idiocy in his head. They'd had a moment; he was sure of it. But he'd got in his head about it and ended up with Sebastien thinking he was taking the piss out of him or something.

Sebastien had started his job working as a junior physiotherapist, and as Nathan had predicted, they'd barely seen each other since.

If he wanted a chance to put things right between them, he needed to set Sebastien straight. Or rather, clarify that he, Nathan, was very much not.

Was it even worth trying, though? Sebastien had only been single for just over over a week, and sure, he'd noticed the spark of attraction in Seb's eyes, but Nathan wasn't prepared to be a fling—not with him. He didn't think his heart could take it.

Looking around his childhood bedroom, he found himself momentarily thrown back in time to when they were kids, lying upside down with his head hanging off Nathan's bed, giggling as they planned a prank on his sister. He was being an idiot. Of course being open with Sebastien was worth it—Nate wanted him in his life even if they could only ever be friends, and he owed him a damn apology for the way he'd left things.

From his bedroom window, he saw Seb step out of his front door and start a series of stretches. Of course, as a physio, he'd be diligent about proper warm-ups. It was ideal really, as it gave Nathan just enough time to bolt down the stairs and throw his trainers on, ignoring the twinge in his shoulder as he raced out to catch Sebastien before he took off.

"Wait up!" he shouted after Sebastien, who had just started to jog slowly down the road.

To his immense relief, Sebastien slowed to a stop.

"Nate," he said with an uneasy smile. "Are you sure you're okay to be out running?"

"I'm fine. I promise to actually take it easy this time. Besides, you can't avoid me forever if we're training together, and I don't want to let Marie down."

"I wasn't avoiding you, it's just I've been incredibly busy with the new job and—"

"And all the other things you've filled your time with to avoid me," Nathan finished for him.

Sebastien laughed. "Okay, fine. Maybe I was avoiding you a tiny bit. Just a smidgen. But can you blame me?"

"Nah, I get it. You think I was being a dick the other day. It happens."

"You were being a dick, Nate," Sebastien insisted. "You can't, like, pretend at attraction you don't feel. It's...mean."

"Mean?" Nathan snarked. "God, how will I recover from that scorcher?"

"Shut up," Sebastien said, a small smile trying to break free.

"Besides, no one was pretending anything."

Sebastien stumbled on a raised paving stone. Nathan reached out to steady him, but Sebastien shook him off. "So what, you're suddenly bi-curious or something?"

"Not curious, and not suddenly." Nathan shrugged.

Sebastien whirled to face him. "Since when?"

"I mean, always, I guess. But I didn't really act on it until college. Are we running, or...?"

"No. We are going to stand right here on this pavement, and you are going to explain why you never said anything. I thought we were close? Did I do something that made you think you couldn't tell me? It was my embarrassing crush, wasn't it? You probably thought I'd, like, try to jump you or something. But, Nate, we're friends, I'd have been there for you."

Sebastien looked like he was spiralling. Nathan reacted, pulling him into a tight hug. "You didn't do anything wrong, Seb."

"But you didn't think you could tell me?"

Nathan sighed. "We never really talked about relationship stuff. At all." That had been mostly by design on Nathan's part; he didn't want to hear about Seb being with other people.

"I guess after Ang, I figured... And then I assumed you wouldn't want to hear about, you know, gay stuff." Sebastien's voice was small and uncertain, so unlike the strong, self-assured man Nathan knew him to be.

"Actually pretty into hearing about gay stuff," Nathan joked.

Sebastien let out a slightly watery-sounding laugh. "You're probably going to regret saying that. I'm going to start bringing you all my drama now."

Nathan arched a brow. "And is there drama?"

Sebastien shrugged. "Not really. Just post-breakup stuff, you know? Trying to put myself back out there, but the apps feel like a minefield after nearly two years without having to go through that whole dance."

A surge of jealousy shot through Nathan at the idea of Sebastien hooking up. He tried to tamp it down.

"Right," he replied. "Is that what you've been busy with this week, then?"

Sebastien's laugh was brighter this time. "No, Nathan. I started a new job, remember? I have genuinely been busy with it—the shift work is a lot to get used to."

"Are you enjoying it, though?"

Sebastien sighed. He started to jog again, and Nathan joined him, slow and steady, determined not to hurt himself further.

"It's not exactly my dream job," Sebastien said. "The people are decent, and I'm sure I'll learn a lot."

"Hardly a ringing endorsement."

They picked up their pace slightly as they continued around the neighbourhood, passing Nathan's favourite pub, which he realised he hadn't set foot in since landing back in London.

"Dar—my ex reached out to me this week. His physio is moving to Canada and selling her practice. He thinks I should take it over."

Nathan pushed down the pesky jealousy that was threatening to rise up again. "What did you say?"

"That I'd think about it. It would be an incredible opportunity, but I don't think I can afford to front the cost of opening my own clinic, and I wouldn't be able to keep my job."

"But you want to do it?" Nathan asked.

Sebastien nodded. "I do, it just...feels like cheating the system though, like a shortcut to my goals that I haven't really earned. Working with athletes at that level isn't something you're supposed to get to do when you're this new."

"You can do it, though, Sebastien. You'd be great. Would it be weird, though? With your ex?"

"I don't think so. Darius isn't—I mean... Fuck."

Nathan nearly tripped over his own feet. There was only one Darius coming up in the pro circuit, and everyone had heard of him. The poised, part-Ethiopian aristocrat being hailed as the next great British marathoner. He was a Marquess, son of a Duke, and the press loved him. There wasn't a chance in hell Nathan would ever be able to measure up to that.

"I can see you connecting the dots, Nate," Sebastien said. "And, obviously, well, he's not out, so please..."

That snapped Nate out of his spiral. "I would never."

Sebastien nodded and fell silent as he continued to run.

"Is that why you split up?" Nate asked.

Sebastien shrugged. "Sort of, definitely part of it, but some things just run their course, you know?"

Nathan nodded sagely, but he didn't know, not really. All of his relationships had burned out in spectacular and dramatic fashion. But that wasn't Sebastien. It made sense that he'd stay friends with his ex. He was exactly the type of person who could do that; kind to a fault, always putting everyone else's needs before his own.

Some semblance of balance had been restored between them. Over the next week, Nathan joined Seb for either an evening run or a gentle walk with Mabel every day. They grew closer, falling back into the easy friendship Nathan remembered from school. It was better now, though—they'd both had more experiences and formed opinions about the world. They'd grown up, and Nathan couldn't help but think they'd grown to complement each other perfectly.

Nathan's shoulder was still bothering him as they ran on Friday night, and as they got to the halfway point of their second lap of the area, a cloud opened overhead, unleashing a summer downpour that drenched them to the bone. They darted home quickly, no longer talking as they raced the rain.

Without discussion, they headed for Sebastien's house. Sebastien arched a judgemental brow at the way Nathan was cradling his arm once again and led him straight upstairs—if Nathan hadn't known that was where he kept all his physio books and equipment, he'd have been more excited by it.

They peeled off their wet clothes, and Sebastien tossed Nathan a pair of joggers to throw on while he tugged on a pair of his own and a worn, slightly too tight T-shirt. It was suspiciously familiar.

"Why do you have a shirt from the under sixteens county track and field championships? I don't remember you being there, and I went every year."

Sebastien flushed. "Just let me look at your shoulder."

Nathan obliged, but he didn't drop it. Because in that moment, he knew. He knew his feelings weren't one-sided. That was *his* shirt.

"When did you steal it?"

With a soft huff, Sebastien replied, "Last year of sixth form, just before exams. You were already off in America, and I was over to see Angie."

And suddenly, Nathan's high was completely doused by that familiar spark of jealousy.

"I don't want you to get the wrong idea here," Sebastien said as his fingers ghosted over Nathan's muscular back. Nathan's fragile ego could barely stand to hear any more. "I cared about your sister, even thought she was really pretty. I wasn't trying to use her."

"I know. I didn't—"

"But I never wanted her the way I wanted you."

Nathan's breath caught in his throat. "Past tense?"

"Not exclusively."

"So if I were to do this—" Nathan leaned forwards so his lips were just a hairsbreadth away from Sebastien's. "—it wouldn't be unwelcome?"

"Not at all," Sebastien breathed.

"Good," Nathan said before he closed the minuscule distance between them, pressing his lips against Sebastien's. Sebastien's tongue darted out, teasing the seam of Nathan's lips, and he opened eagerly to him.

The hand Sebastien still had resting on Nathan's side gripped him harder, pulling him forwards as they explored each other's mouths.

Nathan kissed along Sebastien's jaw and around the shell of his ear before tangling his hands in his hair and returning to plunder his mouth, trying to pour years and years of longing into a single kiss.

When they finally parted, he sighed. "You have no idea how long I've wanted that."

Sebastien laughed. "No longer than I have, I'm sure."

"I think we should probably try it again, just so I know this isn't a dream."

Instead of saying anything, Sebastien surged forward, kissing Nathan deeply.

Chapter 5
Sebastien

6 WEEKS TO THE SCOTLAND 100

If someone had told sixteen-year-old Sebastien that kissing Nathaniel Steele was a thing he'd one day be allowed to do whenever he wanted, he'd have thought they were delusional, but for the past week, that had been his reality.

There was a tiny voice in the back of his head telling him this was dangerous. Nate had already said he had no plans to stay in London, and Sebastien wasn't sure he could handle the heartbreak of watching him leave again. He tried to push it from his mind, though, because right now, as they were...it was everything Sebastien had ever wanted. Well, nearly.

They were cuddled up together in a corner booth in their local pub. They'd been for a run together when Sebastien got home from his early shift and had parted only when Nate insisted on going home to shower and change. Even though it was just their local, it felt like more than just going out for a pint with a friend.

It felt like a date.

Nathan wound their hands together on top of the table, and Sebastien's heart fluttered. He'd never been able to do this, to sit and hold hands so openly in public. Darius had been his only long-term relationship, and they'd always taken care to present themselves as friends when they went out; you never knew when a reporter would be lurking, trying to catch a scoop. He let himself lean into Nathan as he took a gulp of his pint. It felt nice. Comfortable.

"Have you made a decision?" Nathan asked. "About work?"

Sebastien sighed. He'd already started to hate his job—the hours were terrible, the work was menial at best, and any hope he'd had of it being a great learning experience to start off with had gone out the window. The idea Darius had planted in his head about running his own clinic, with a client list full of professional athletes, was looking better every minute. He was scared, though, and there was no way he could afford it.

"I told him I'd meet up with him," Sebastien replied. He felt Nate's hand tense in his slightly and grinned. "Why, Nathaniel, are you jealous?"

"No," Nate grumbled, taking a swig of his pint. "I just don't like that he hurt you, and now you have to go play nice, but I don't want to tell you not to do it because I know it's a great opportunity."

Sebastien leaned in and kissed him. "He didn't hurt me, not really. You don't have to worry." Seb let his hand trail over Nathan's thigh, tracing the inseam of his jeans. "I'm a big boy, I can handle myself."

"Yeah?" Nathan said with a sharp intake of breath.

Sebastien hummed. "Are your parents home?"

For a moment, Sebastien was transported back in time, asking a question like that felt embarrassingly childish, but Nate didn't seem to notice his momentary lapse in confidence.

"They're out for the evening. Dinner and a show with Ang," he replied.

Necking his pint, Sebastien grinned. "What on earth are we still doing here then?"

Sebastien's heart skipped a beat as he watched Nathan drain his drink, Adam's apple bobbing as he swallowed. They both knew what was coming next, and in many ways it felt like his whole life had been leading up to this moment. Nathan took his hand and led him out the door of their local pub, down the streets they'd played on as children, then kissed him soundly on the doorstep before pulling him into the house that had been like a second home to him as far back as he could remember.

Nathan's room was almost exactly as Sebastien remembered, though he hadn't been here in years. Not since the day he'd broken up with Angie, when he'd run from the room after their conversation, cried into her absent brother's pillow, then stolen a T-shirt from his drawer before running from the house. Since that moment, he'd avoided the house. Even on the rare occasion when they'd seen each other during summer breaks, Sebastien had always insisted on neutral territory or his place; anything that would help him maintain the careful distance he'd put in place to protect his heart.

He didn't need to do that now.

He turned from his study of the room to look at Nathan, who was sitting on the edge of his bed, wringing his hands. Something about the vulnerability in his posture struck a chord in Sebastien.

"There's no pressure, Nate." He was trying to be encouraging, suddenly aware that he didn't know how much experience Nate had with men, and the last thing he wanted to do was push him into something he wasn't ready for.

Nathan smiled sheepishly at him. "It's not that. I...I'm just not sure what happens next."

"Like, physically, or...?"

"No, you twit." Nathan laughed. "I mean, what do you like? Or, er, what do you want to do?"

Sebastien settled next to Nate on the edge of the bed. "Well, right this second I want to kiss you. But if you're asking about after that, I'm vers."

Nathan smiled. "Me too, but, Sebastien…I really want you to fuck me tonight."

Lust shot through Sebastien's body at Nathan's proclamation. "Yeah," he choked out. "That sounds brilliant." *Brilliant?* Sebastien's cheeks flushed. God, he had no game whatsoever. It was a damn good thing Nathan was already used to his inability to ever say the right thing.

Nathan was grinning at him, though, and leaning in. Kissing his jaw, his neck, the shell of his ear. "Yeah, brilliant," he whispered as he snaked a hand under Sebastien's shirt.

"I was tested two weeks ago, after…" Sebastien trailed off as Nathan pushed him down on the bed, climbing over him. "And I'm on PrEP."

"I haven't been with anyone since my last test," Nathan rocked back on his heels and shucked his shirt.

Sebastien had seen Nathan shirtless plenty of times in the past few weeks. He'd touched the planes of his muscles and dug his fingers in to work out the tight knots, but nothing could have prepared him for the sight of Nathan straddling him shirtless, lips kiss-bitten and hard cock straining in his joggers.

Sebastien was so hard he ached as Nathan ground against him. He needed to touch him. Needed to taste him. He reached out, grasping for Nate's hips and pulling him in for a filthy kiss as he yanked down the joggers, touching his hardening cock lightly at first as he worked his own jeans down to his ankles. Nate's hands were on him in a flash, his caresses matching the languid pace of his tongue against Sebastien's nipple as he teased him. A groan sounded in the room, and Sebastien honestly couldn't be sure whether the sound had come from him or Nate.

Too clouded with lust to voice anything coherently, he tapped Nate's thigh and pulled him forwards, trying to mime what he wanted.

"You're going to have to use your words, Seb." Nate chuckled as he tugged gently at Sebastien's sac, eliciting another low groan.

"Come on, baby. Tell me what you want me to do."

Sebastien huffed and shimmied himself down on the bed. "Sit on my fucking face, Nate," he groaned out.

Nathan stilled.

Sebastien froze as well. "Or not. I mean, if you're not into..."

"Shhhh." Nathan placed a finger over his lips. "Let me savour the moment all my teenage fantasies come true."

The tension broke between them, and they dissolved into giggles for a moment before Sebastien gripped Nathan's thighs and slid himself underneath. He spread his cheeks and took a moment to admire the tight hole before him. Nathan had joked about his teenage fantasies, but he had no idea the level of fantasy fulfilment Sebastien was reaching in this moment. He stopped thinking and let his most carnal instincts take over, claiming Nate with his tongue.

Nate's moans echoed around the room and his thighs shook as Sebastien feasted, alternating between flattening his tongue over the rosebud and spearing it into him. His own cock leaked and throbbed but he ignored it, focused on the task before him.

"Fuck, fuck. Stop." Nate groaned, gripping the base of his cock as he rolled to the side. He fumbled in the nightstand before tossing a small bottle of lube to Sebastien. "I don't want to come until you're inside me."

Seb stilled. "Do you have condoms?"

"We don't need one do we?" Nate asked, eyes wide with faux-innocence.

Seb nearly choked on his tongue. *Talk about wish fulfilment.* "If you're sure..."

Nathan grinned. "Fuck me raw, Seb."

Sebastien moved quickly after that. He coated his fingers in lube and tugged Nate back over, using his fingers to replace his tongue. He stretched Nate in a practiced, efficient manner despite his desperation, before dribbling a liberal amount of the lube over his own cock.

Nate shimmied down, gripping Sebastien's shoulders as he lowered himself. He paused, wincing slightly, and Sebastien tried to catalogue the photographs in the room to stop himself from coming embarrassingly soon. Nate continued slowly, a deep sigh leaving him as he seated himself fully. Their eyes met, and Sebastien wasn't sure if he was going to laugh or cry—all he knew was that Nathan Steele was his now, and he was never going to let him go again.

He linked their fingers together as Nate rose and began riding him in earnest. The air crackled with electricity, but Sebastien's focus was absolute. There was nothing but him and Nate—an infinite loop of dreams, fantasies, and reality that blended together in his head and solidified into one very simple truth.

He was in love.

Sebastien surged up to capture Nathan's lips with his, determined not to blurt out a mid-coitus love confession absurdly early in their not-even-a-relationship. He took Nate's cock in his hand and jerked it roughly between them as Nathan's movements started to stutter.

Seconds after Nate's passage clenched around him, his own orgasm followed. Colours exploded in his vision as he released inside him, and they collapsed backwards on the bed, Nathan's weight pushing him down into the mattress.

They lay together in silence for a moment, sweat cooling on their skin and cum leaking onto the sheets. Then Nate rolled off Sebastien and the spell broke.

"We should probably get cleaned up," Nate said with a soft smile.

"Yeah." Sebastien nodded. "We should."

"Shower?" Nate asked, and Sebastien couldn't help but dive in to kiss him again.

Showering led to touching, and touching led to another round of soft, slow sex, which then somehow led to a competitive pillow fight while they changed Nate's sheets. A pillow fight that ended in sleepy kisses before they curled up, whispering to each other under the crisp, clean sheets until they fell asleep in each other's arms.

Chapter 6

Nathan

6 WEEKS TO THE SCOTLAND 100

"Wake up, loser, there's pancakes." A screeching voice broke through the sleepy haze Nathan was enjoying. If he hadn't been able to feel the weight of Sebastien beside him, he'd have been convinced last night was nothing more than an elaborate dream.

It wasn't like he hadn't had those exact dreams before.

Sebastien was there, though, snoring softly next to him, and all he wanted to do was pull him into his arms, wake him up with soft, slow kisses and enjoy a morning together. But nope, his damn sister was in the house and screeching at the top of her bloody lungs.

Sebastien started to stir as the least delicate footsteps of all time thundered up the stairs. They only had seconds to react.

"Sebastien," Nathan whispered in his ear, "Angie's going to come through that door in about five seconds."

"Fuck." Sebastien's eyes flew open and he darted out of the bed and Nathan's arms, then stumbled into the bathroom.

Nathan couldn't help but feel disappointed, like Sebastien's fear of discovery proved this was just a hookup to him. Like it cheapened what he'd thought they had together.

"Nate, hurry up. Dad won't let us start without you and I've got shit to do today," Angie shouted as she burst through the door.

"Ever heard of knocking?" Nate drawled as he pulled the duvet up higher over his chest.

Angie rolled her eyes before she spotted the pile of dirty sheets in the corner and a sly grin came over her face. "Oh my god, Nathan, did you bring a hookup back to our parents' house?" She laughed. "At least every time I think my life has hit rock bottom, you're here to remind me there's further to fall."

"Shut up, Angie." That was harsh, but Ang had always been like that with him. Never one to mince words for the sake of his ego, constantly needing to dig the knife in further and remind him of his failures. She'd say that was what siblings were for, but Nathan was convinced there was an edge to her insults, something sharper and deeper than she'd ever admit.

"Is she still here?" She cackled. "Hiding in the wardrobe maybe?" She threw open his closet door. "Or maybe the bathroom?"

She started to walk towards it, and Nathan was helpless to stop her. "Ang, please," he sighed.

But then Sebastien threw open the bathroom door, clad only in a towel, with a shit-eating grin on his face.

"Angie, god, it's been ages. It's so good to see you," he said as he pulled Nathan's shell-shocked sister into a hug.

Angie spluttered, and Nathan couldn't help the smug satisfaction he felt. "Are you—but he—I —"

"Did I hear you say pancakes?"

"Yes?" she replied tentatively.

Sebastien have her another of his easy smiles. "We'll be down in a few, tell your dad there's no need to wait though." He winked.

As soon as she was out the door, Sebastien deflated. "I'm so sorry. I didn't want to out you, but then she was going to open the door and—"

"Seb, it's fine. I don't care. Angie's known for years how obsessed I am with you."

Sebastien arched a brow. "Obsessed?"

"Mmm. Obsessed with your smile." He kissed him on the lips. "Your eyes." He kissed his temple. "Your abs." He kissed down his chest. "And now..." He pushed Sebastien down onto the bed, lowering himself to kiss his way up his inner thigh. "Now, I'm really fucking obsessed with your cock."

Nathan inhaled deeply, committing the scent of Sebastien to memory as he dragged his tongue over the tip of his rapidly swelling cock.

"Nate, we said we'd be right down. The pancakes."

"Pancakes can wait."

Nate sucked him into his mouth and Sebastien moaned, the sound vibrated through him. He was right, they didn't have much time, so Nate pulled out every trick in his book.

The pancakes had gone cold and Sebastien's parents had left for the day by the time they made it down to the kitchen.

·♥·♥·♥·♥·♥·

The work week dragged for Nathan. He still hadn't found a job, and he could only fling his CV out into the ether so many times before it started to feel absolutely futile. On top of the ongoing failure of his job search, Angie was always around, and now, as well as being a general pain and constant reminder of his failures, she was also a massive cock-block.

Sebastien's hours were long and his job was stressful, but instead of being able to curl up together in the evenings, they were resigned to uncomfortable silence and stilted conversation at Nathan's or being pulled into family game nights at Sebastien's. The only one having a great time that week was Mabel, who was seriously benefitting from Nathan's need to get away from his sister, with walkies to the park becoming a much more frequent feature of the day.

Tonight, Sebastien had once again joined him and Mabel on their evening walk. They strolled hand in hand as Seb told Nathan about his day. It was becoming increasingly apparent that the work wasn't fulfilling, and though it had only been a couple of weeks, it hurt to see Sebastien so down about a subject he'd once been so passionate about.

"I met up with Darius," he blurted out as they rounded the corner, entering the familiar park.

"That's great." Nathan kept his voice steady, really trying to be cool about it. He bent down to let Mabel off her lead and tossed a ball for her. "What did he say?"

"We went to see the clinic, and god, it would be so cool, Nate. It's small but busy. There are three elite runners and a couple of juniors who are regular clients that he knows of."

Nathan didn't trust himself to speak. The idea of Sebastien working on his ex regularly didn't exactly fill him with joy, but he could see how badly he wanted this, and he wanted it for him too.

"The problem," Sebastien continued, "is that I'd need to come up with the capital, at least for the initial purchase, and then I wouldn't be able to even think about paying myself a salary until I'd paid off a decent chunk of it."

Nathan nodded. "So, what would it take for you to get this off the ground?"

"They're asking four hundred thousand, and honestly, that's probably underpriced for a quick sale, but I can't afford to buy a business. I'm twenty-three years old; I've got, like, a couple grand in savings."

Nathan wrapped an arm around Sebastien's waist as he clipped Mabel's lead back on for the walk home. "There's loans, and I'm sure we can cobble together some family support."

"We?"

Nathan smiled. "I'm going to help you figure this out. You deserve it, Sebastien. You deserve everything."

Sebastien smiled at him and leaned in for a soft kiss. Yeah, Nathan was going to do whatever he could to help Sebastien get this, even if it meant he might lose him to Darius *bloody* Hewitt.

The next day, while everyone was at work, Nathan was busy with something other than job applications for the first time. He'd asked Sebastien for the details of the investment requirements for the clinic and had been sent a massive file that Sebastien had sheepishly admitted he couldn't make heads or tails of. For the first time since graduating, Nathan was putting his business degree to use as he combed through valuations and financial statements, setting things out neatly in a spreadsheet to sort out exactly how much Sebastien would need and the best approach to raising that investment.

It was clear that the clinic was successful and had a strong client list. It would be an incredible business, and between the central location, the steady client base, and the size of the space itself, Seb had been right that the asking price was more than fair. But Nathan didn't think there was much chance of securing such a large business loan. Not for an unproven new graduate.

He'd asked Sebastien to come over after work so he could show him, but now, he wasn't sure he wanted to. He couldn't bear to be the one to crush Sebastien's dreams. The knowledge that he couldn't do anything to support Seb himself gnawed at him. His lack of gainful employment had become even more of a sore point for Nathan since he'd discovered that Seb's ex was not only a professional athlete, but an aristocrat with generational wealth and a clear desire to stay in his life despite their supposedly mutual breakup.

Nathan knew he needed to get a handle on his jealous streak. He didn't want to push Seb away, it was just that he found it all a bit off that Darius had even suggested this. Surely he wasn't so out of touch that he hadn't realised Seb wouldn't have the funds to buy a successful business fresh out of uni?

Maybe if Darius wanted to help Sebastien so damn badly he could put his money where his mouth was. Meddling prick.

Oh no. That was the solution, wasn't it?

Nathan hesitated for just a moment, because if he did this, if it worked out, it would mean keeping Sebastien in his ex's orbit indefinitely. The choice was easy, though; he cared about Seb's happiness way more than he cared about his own insecurities.

He opened his Instagram and sent a follow request to Darius Hewitt, and he was surprised when it was approved in seconds. A quick scroll of the page showed a lot of bland running-related content, but he sent a DM anyway, asking for a call to talk about Sebastien. Nathan nearly jumped out of his skin when his phone started to buzz almost immediately.

It wasn't Darius Hewitt though, but a young female voice on the other end.

"Care to explain why you're threatening my brother?" she asked.

Nathan spluttered. "I'm not threatening him, I need to speak with him."

"Oh sure, that seems likely."

He supposed he could understand her perspective on this. As a family, they'd been through the wringer in the tabloids years ago, but he didn't think his message had been especially threatening in tone.

"Seriously, it's about physiotherapy. He recommended my, er, business partner for a job and I have no contact details for him."

"Your business partner." The scepticism was evident in her voice. "Fine," she replied with a huff. "I'll pass him your details, but even a hint of blackmail or funny business and I will hunt you down."

He imagined it was meant to be scary, but the girl couldn't have been more than fifteen and he'd dealt with his own genuinely terrifying sister his whole life.

"Thank you. I appreciate it."

"Whatever," she said before the line went dead.

A couple of hours later, Nathan was on the underground making his way to Battersea Park to meet Darius Hewitt. It was surreal. A few months ago—hell, a few weeks ago—he'd have been thrilled to meet British marathoning's up-and-coming star, but today he was just irritated with the man. Nathan was pretty confident at this point that Darius was trying to orchestrate a reconciliation with Sebastien. Of course he was; Sebastien was incredible, and he couldn't fathom anyone not wanting to be with him. Nate could feel his thoughts meandering, if he wanted to make this work for Seb then he needed to focus on the pitch he'd prepared. As his stop approached, he mentally ran back over the numbers.

Nathan didn't know the area well, but it was easy to navigate to the small café near the lake—every park in London seemed to have a similar design to it. He clocked Hewitt immediately. His bronze skin and patrician looks that featured on adverts throughout the city felt unusually poised for the small café. He was one of the few patrons sitting inside the building, as others opted to enjoy the sunshine from the many lakeside picnic tables. Hewitt rose as he entered and moved in to shake his hand. It all felt very formal.

"You must be Nathan," he said with an uneasy smile. "Can I get you a drink?"

Nathan mumbled a greeting and a request for a black americano, taking a moment to settle himself at the table as Darius went to the counter to order. He pulled out his laptop with the projections he'd drawn up earlier that morning and nervously tapped his fingers on the table. He couldn't believe he was doing this. Maybe it was all a mistake. What if Sebastien was angry with him for meddling? Or what if he'd downplayed the breakup and it was all much worse than he thought? Nathan hesitated, on the verge of packing his laptop away, but just then, Darius returned, passing him a steaming hot americano in a brown paper cup. Nathan inhaled. He loved coffee; something about the scent always settled him.

"Selena said you're Sebastien's business partner?" Darius said.

Nathan flushed. "That may have been a slight exaggeration."

Darius studied him. It was unnerving—he was incredibly poised, making Nathan feel like an absolute mess in comparison. It was completely impossible to imagine that Sebastien would settle for Nathan when his last relationship had been with someone so...together.

"I recognised you the second you walked in, you know?" Darius mused. "Seb used to talk about you non-stop. You're a runner, right? Went to America on a scholarship?"

"Yeah, Harvard. The eight hundred was my speciality," Nathan replied. It wasn't the most comfortable topic for him, but at least it was common ground in a way. Common ground that wasn't Nathan's not-quite boyfriend.

"Nice. I never was much of a sprinter. You still training?"

Nathan shrugged. "Not really. Seb and I are running together a bit, but not trying to go pro or anything."

Darius nodded along. "Fair enough. Sebastien must like having you around again."

"What's that supposed to mean?" Nathan asked, suddenly defensive.

Darius squinted at him. "Only that I know he missed you." He cocked his head to the side. "What did you think I meant?"

Avoiding the question, Nathan took a sip of his coffee. He could feel the heat creeping up his neck.

"No way," Darius whispered, staring Nathan down. "You're together, aren't you?"

Nathan spluttered as he tried to find a way to respond, but Darius was still talking. "Good. Sebastien's been obsessed with you forever. Even I could see that, and believe me, social cues are not my forte."

"You're not upset?" Nathan asked quietly.

Darius shook his head, but he was wringing his hands, and Nathan wasn't sure what to expect when he began speaking again. "I don't want to lose Sebastien from my life," he said, casually confirming all of Nathan's fears. "But I don't want to get back together, if that's what you're worried about."

Of bloody course that was what Nathan was worried about.

"I... Look, I don't have a lot of friends, and I know it's weird to want to be friends with an ex, but Sebastien and I were good like that, before the relationship stuff got in the way. It's why I mentioned the clinic—because I know he'd love it, and at least then we'd see each other."

There was something in his tone that made Nathan, who considered himself pretty cynical at the best of times, believe him.

"He can't afford it," he blurted out with none of the professionalism he'd intended for this meeting.

Darius looked genuinely confused, and Nathan had to stifle a laugh. Bloody rich fuckers, so out of touch with the real world.

"Why didn't he just say that?" he asked.

Nathan sighed. "Because he wants it so badly, he hates his new job, and you basically dangled everything he wants for himself just out of his reach."

A contrite look passed over Darius's face. "I didn't mean to make things harder for him. Is there anything I can do to fix this?"

"Well," Nathan said, back on surer footing, "I've actually got a couple of thoughts on that if you don't mind taking a look?"

That evening, Nathan and Sebastien were blissfully alone at Seb's place. They'd cooked together, shared a bottle of red wine over dinner, and were just retreating to the sitting room when Nathan got a call from an unknown number. He answered quickly, mouthing an apology to Sebastien. He expected it to be Darius, ringing to let him know his thoughts on the proposal he'd made that afternoon, but it wasn't Darius.

It was a recruiter.

Nathan hadn't heard back about any of the applications he'd submitted over the past few weeks, so it honestly startled him to get a call, especially so late.

Apparently it was urgent, though. They had a client interested in his profile who wanted to interview him tomorrow morning. It was the perfect job on paper, working on legacy projects for the Commonwealth Games. The only catch? The job was in Glasgow.

Nathan hadn't set any location parameters on his job search, but had always figured he'd end up staying near enough to London, regardless. It was where the majority of jobs in his field were, after all. He certainly hadn't considered the idea of moving to Scotland. Especially now.

He looked over at Sebastien, sipping his tea as he waited patiently for him on the couch. Could they survive long distance? Things were just starting to grow between them, and the idea of being separated honestly broke Nathan's heart.

Still, he confirmed the interview—a video call, thankfully—for the next morning, then joined Seb on the couch, his mood in total flux.

"Everything okay?" Sebastien asked.

Nathan smiled. "Just an interview for tomorrow morning."

A grin split Sebastien's face. "That's brilliant, Nathan!"

"Yeah, I-I guess it is. It's just...the job's up in Glasgow."

Nathan thought he saw Sebastien's bright expression slip for a moment, but it was so quick he might have imagined it.

"Glasgow's a great city." Sebastien gave him an easy smile.

"Yeah," Nathan replied. But inside, he was screaming at Seb to tell him not to do the interview. To tell him to stay in London. To tell him to stay with him.

Chapter 7
Sebastien

4 WEEKS TO THE SCOTLAND 100

He should have been happy for Nathan. Obviously, that was what you were supposed to do when good things happened for your friends. Be happy for them.

He couldn't, though, because the job offer Nathan had received after obviously nailing his interview would take him away from Sebastien, away from whatever they were to each other now that was definitely more than friends, but maybe not quite as much more as Sebastien had hoped.

He could already feel him pulling away, putting distance between them. It wasn't that they didn't see each other; they did. Nearly every day in fact. Nathan seemed distant, though, like he was holding back.

Although he was exhausted from yet another long shift, Sebastien made his way over to Nathan's for the training run they'd planned. His shoulder was doing better, at least enough that he could run without risk of further injury. It was yet another thing Sebastien felt he was losing; Nathan didn't need him anymore if he was healing, and with his potential move coming up, it seemed likely that the end of whatever was happening between them was nigh.

As he waited at Nathan's door, he planned what he needed to say. He was primed to confront him, ready to force a discussion about feelings, but it wasn't Nathan who answered, it was Angie.

"Sebastien," she breathed as she yanked open the door.

Sebastien nervously massaged his own neck as he replied. "Angie." He hadn't had a conversation one-on-one with her in years. Not since they'd broken up, really.

"Nathan isn't back yet."

"Oh, okay. I'll just..."

"Do you want a cuppa while you wait?" she offered right as Sebastien was finishing with "...head home until he's back."

Sebastien flushed. "Yeah, sure. It'd be nice to catch up."

It was awkward. That was the only way he could describe it, really. On no planet did Sebastien want to sit and drink tea with the girl he'd dated in high school, whose brother he was now hooking up with. Just no.

"So, you and Nathan finally happened."

Oh, good, this sounded like a fun conversation.

"He always does get whatever he wants in the end." She sighed.

Sebastien frowned. "What's that supposed to mean?"

She laughed sardonically. "Oh, he loves to play the 'woe is me, living with my parents' card, but seriously, he's got a great degree, no debt, and a hot boyfriend. The arsehole could swan dive from a rockface and still find a way to land on his feet."

"I don't think we're boyfriends," Sebastien replied. He was aware there was a deeper meaning behind what Angie was saying, but he needed to clarify that point. "He's going to leave anyway. To Glasgow."

"So you'll be long distance. You're definitely boyfriends, Sebastien. Don't be naive."

Sebastien felt his ire growing. This had been half the problem with dating Angie when he was younger; she couldn't stand to let anyone else be right, always had to have the last word. Of course, the other half of their issues had mostly been the fact that she was very much female and Sebastien was very much gay.

"I'm not naive, Ang. Maybe you shouldn't try to...to whatever the fucking equivalent of mansplaining my own life to me is."

"Did you ever care about me at all? Or was I just a stand-in for what you really wanted?" she asked suddenly, causing Sebastien's freewheeling anger to careen to a halt.

"Ang, it's been years. We were kids."

She fixed him with a stare. "Answer the question, Sebastien."

It wasn't an easy answer, though. Sebastien didn't think he'd been using Ang to get to Nathan, but his feelings had been so tied up in all of his confusion about life and his future and his sexuality that it had been hard to tell where one ended and the other began.

"I wasn't using you to get to Nate," he said with slightly more certainty than he felt. "But I think...I think I might have been unfair to you anyway."

Angie sighed. "We were teenagers. Nobody goes into a relationship at fifteen for the right reasons. I just... Well, I didn't think you and Nathan would ever actually happen. When we first broke up I thought you blamed me for that, and that was why we stopped being friends but the other day... seeing you together, I realised, maybe I've been wrong. Maybe I've blamed my brother for years for something that never had anything to do with him."

"You mean our breakup?"

Ang nodded. "And you stopped being my friend, Sebastien. I thought maybe this year, when I heard you were seeing someone, things might have settled enough for us to hang out. You've barely spoken to me in years, but every summer when he came home, you looked at Nathan like the sun shone out of his arse."

"It kind of does," Sebastien replied cheekily.

"Look, Seb, I'd like to be friends again, but I don't ever—and I mean *ever*—want to hear anything about my brother's arse."

Sebastien sniggered. "That's fair, I guess." He took another sip of his cooling tea. "Why are you back, by the way? I never did get around to asking."

"Seb, the last time I saw you, you were dressed in a towel, hiding in my brother's en suite. It wasn't prime chatting time."

Sebastien shrugged, waiting for her to answer.

"Caught my boyfriend cheating. Had to get out, so I came back here."

"I'm sorry. Are you okay?"

Angie laughed. "I'll live. I don't think I'll bounce back into another relationship quite as quickly as you and Nathan have, but I'll get over it."

"It's not a relationship," Sebastien argued weakly.

Angie cocked her head. "You really believe that, don't you?"

"Of course. We aren't boyfriends."

A choked sound came from the doorway, and Sebastien whipped his head around to see Nathan standing there with a bag at his feet and dejected look on his face.

"Aren't we?" he whispered.

Angie slid off the stool, slinking out of the room like the shit-stirrer she was, pausing only to whisper something in Nathan's ear that Sebastien wished he could have heard.

And then they were alone.

Staring at each other, with Sebastien's proclamation hanging between them.

"I-I wanted to talk to you about something," Nathan said.

Sebastien buried his face in his hands. "Oh god, are you breaking things off?"

"Thought we weren't boyfriends," Nathan countered.

"I mean, we aren't. We haven't... Do you want to be?" Sebastien asked incredulously.

"Of course I do, Seb," Nathan said simply.

Sebastien's brain wasn't keeping pace. "But the job... You'll have to move and—"

"Long distance is a thing. I can travel back on weekends sometimes, and you can come up. I think we can make it work."

"But my shifts... Sometimes I'll have to work weekends, and it's so unpredictable right now..."

There was an unreadable look on Nathan's face, but he was shifting back and forth like he was bursting to tell Sebastien something. It was a tell he'd had since they were kids. He'd never been able to keep a gift secret for long, often resulting in spoiled Christmas surprises that their families still joked about even now.

"Okay, out with it," Sebastien demanded.

Nathan bit his lip. "I don't know what you're talking about."

"You've been acting shifty for days. I thought you were dumping me, but clearly something else is going on."

"I wasn't dumping you! I'd never."

Sebastien arched a brow and waited for him to spill.

"I think you're going to be able to run that clinic," Nathan said.

Sebastien frowned. "What do you mean? You saw the numbers; there's no way I can afford that. I don't know what Darius was thinking."

"You could if you had an investor."

"But I don't have an investor," Sebastien explained slowly, like he was speaking to a small child.

"You do now." Nathan grinned.

"Who would..." Sebastien let the question die on his lips. There was no way, right? "You didn't."

Nathan took a deep breath. "Please don't be angry. I just took him a business proposal and some projections. It's a solid investment, not a handout."

"Are you pushing this because you're leaving?"

"No. Well, maybe a little bit. I want you to be happy, Seb. And I think doing this with Darius's support could be perfect for you."

"I don't want...I don't want to date him again, Nathan."

Nathan started. "Of course not, and he doesn't want to date you again either."

Okay, that was a good thing, even if it was a slight blow to Sebastien's ego. "Because I want to date you," Sebastien insisted. "I want to be your boyfriend."

A grin took over Nathan's face. "That's perfect." He leaned in to plant a smacking kiss on Sebastien's lips. "'Cause I want to be your boyfriend too."

Everything was moving far too fast. Nathan had signed his contract and had less than a week left in London before he'd be moving to Scotland, and away from Sebastien. Sure, they'd agreed to try the long-distance thing, but Sebastien couldn't help but have his doubts. They'd been long-distance friends for years, and he didn't think they'd done a particularly good job of that—it seemed naive to think they'd be better at it as boyfriends.

Still, he was trying to make Nathan's last few days in London ones to remember. And maybe, just a little bit, hoping the city itself could convince him to stay, something Sebastien himself clearly wasn't enough to do. With only a few days left, it was time to pull out the big guns. He called off sick and turned up at Nathan's door bright and early, earning himself a smirk from Angie as he rushed his boyfriend out of bed and got him to pack an overnight bag. They left Mabel in Angie's care as agreed. Turned out it was useful having her on side.

"Are you going to tell me where we're going?" Nathan groused as he threw his toiletries together.

"Nope," Sebastien replied, popping the P in the most exaggerated manner he could muster.

"At least what I need to bring?"

"Not much. Probably this." Sebastien smirked, rifling through Nathan's nightstand and tossing him the bottle of lube he knew he kept there.

"Wow, my boyfriend is so sophisticated. So romantic. I never know quite what to expect," Nathan deadpanned.

Sebastien pouted. "You asked. Besides, that's not all I have planned."

"You know I'd be into it if it was, right?"

Sebastien marched over to him and flicked him on the nose. "Well, it isn't, because your boyfriend is sophisticated and romantic. So hurry the fuck up before we lose the sophisticated, romantic reservations I made."

"I'm coming, I'm coming," Nathan groused.

Sebastien grinned. "Not y—"

"Don't even say it." Nathan laughed. He planted a firm kiss on Sebastien before swinging his bag over his shoulder and following him through the house and out the door to the Canonbury Overground Station.

"Are you going to tell me yet?" Nathan asked as they tapped their phones and walked through the barriers.

"If you keep asking, I might have to gag you."

There was a moment of silence between them as Seb steered them to the platform for the eastbound Windrush line. While they waited for the train, Nathan leaned in and murmured, "I wouldn't be opposed to that. You know, under the right circumstances."

Sebastien stammered what he hoped was a coherent response, though looking back, there wasn't a chance in hell he'd be able to confirm what he did or did not say as they boarded, and they'd gone two stops before it occurred to him to even check they were going the right direction. Nathan just laughed and wrapped an arm around his shoulders as the train rumbled on through Central London. Sebastien had barely recovered by the time they switched to the Docklands Light Railway. Every time he tried to think of something, his brain seemed to circle back to the image of Nathan, bound and gagged, waiting for him on—no, he needed to focus on wooing. Wooing was the mission of the day, as part of *Operation Convince Nate to Stay in London and Be with Me Forever*. He was still workshopping the name, but the strategy was pretty sound.

Exiting the station, he guided Nathan down the street and parked him at a table in a coffee shop with a massive iced latte and instructions not to move until he was back, which earned him a "Yes, sir" that did funny things to his brain chemistry. He grabbed their bags, though and made a beeline for the hotel.

Just looking around the lobby, he knew he'd made the right choice. It was swanky, very London, but not too much. Definitely the best he could've done on his budget. He dropped the bags off with reception and confirmed the champagne he'd pre-ordered for their room. It was still far too early for check-in, but that was fine—Sebastien had a full day of wooing ahead.

Nathan was waiting at the coffee shop, scrolling on his phone and absentmindedly sipping the dregs of his coffee, which from where Sebastien was standing looked like it was mostly just melted ice at this point. He took a moment to admire him. This man he'd been half in love with all his life. The man he'd felt lucky just to call a friend, and now had to pinch himself on the regular when he thought about the way the word "boyfriend" had come out of Nathan's mouth, so nonchalant, like it was fucking obvious that was what they were.

Nathan's plump lips around the straw did things to Sebastien. The way his Adam's apple bobbed as he tried to suck the last remains of his drink through the paper straw that was deteriorating faster from his assault on it.

Sebastien walked towards him, his pace quickening, then pulled him up out of his chair and into his arms, kissing him firmly as he gently removed the cup from Nathan's hands and placed it in the bin.

"I wasn't done with that," Nathan groused.

"Pretty sure you were just getting room temperature water and bits of paper straw at the end there, baby."

"Maybe I like room temperature water and bits of paper straw."

Seb rolled his eyes. "If I promise to get you another one later, will you get a move on?"

"Do I get to know where we're going?"

"To the river."

"The river." The look on Nathan's face said '*that tells me fuck all, thanks.*'

"Can you just trust me for today?" Sebastien asked.

Nathan took his hand. "I always trust you, Sebastien. Always have, always will."

Chapter 8
Nathan

4 WEEKS TO THE SCOTLAND 100

"Oh my fucking god, this is fast," Nathan exclaimed as the boat sped down the river towards the Thames Barrier. "This is so cool, why have I never done this before?"

He looked over at his boyfriend, and his heart skipped a beat when their eyes met. Seb was looking back at him with a sort of desperate longing that cracked something open inside him.

"London's got a lot to offer, hasn't it?" Sebastien asked, clearly aiming for a level of nonchalance he didn't quite manage. Maybe if Nathan hadn't known him for as long as he had, and if he hadn't spent the majority of his teenage years mapping the micro expressions his face made—like the way his eyes crinkled when he was truly happy or his nose scrunched when he was thinking too hard—maybe he wouldn't have understood. As it was, Nathan was struck by a moment of painful clarity. This wasn't just Sebastien planning a spontaneous date to get them some private time away from their families. This was Seb's attempt to convince him to stay, likely because he still didn't understand that nothing, not his sister, not overly successful exes, and certainly not a six-hour train journey's worth of distance, would be able to convince Nathan to let Sebastien go now that he had him.

As far as Nathan was concerned, they were endgame. It was obvious, though, that he hadn't done enough to show Seb he meant it when he said they'd make it work.

As they reached the Thames Barrier and the tourists around them gawked at the engineering marvel, a testament to human ingenuity that protected London and its millions of inhabitants from the whims of the mighty river, Nathan pulled his boyfriend close and whispered in his ear. "The best thing London has to offer is right here in my arms."

He was rewarded with a blush and a chaste kiss on the lips.

On the return journey, Nathan and Seb disembarked in Greenwich while most others carried on to the docks at Embankment. The speed of the ride had left them both windswept and chilled, but the sun was shining as they walked through the park.

Sebastien paused, and Nathan watched as he lowered his backpack to the ground and started to pull out all the fixings for a classic picnic, chequered blanket included. They settled in, looking back at the city as Sebastien poured prosecco into plastic flutes and handed Nathan an egg and cress sandwich.

As he dug in, Nathan contemplated how to bring it up. But as seemed to be his usual style these days, he ended up just blurting it out in the least sensitive manner possible.

"Is this about me moving?" he asked.

Sebastien sighed and picked at the netting on a pack of wax-covered cheese rounds. "Is it that obvious?"

"A little." Nathan shrugged. "The whole 'look how amazing London is' vibe."

"Yeah, I guess it wasn't the most subtle approach." Sebastien looked contrite.

"No, baby, it's so sweet. I love everything about this day. I just want to make sure you know you don't have to do this. I already want to stay. I'd give anything to just stay here with you, but I can't pass up the only job offer I've had in months. I can't live with my parents and mooch off them forever."

"I know that, I just... I wish you weren't going so far away."

"I told you we'd make it work. Is that...is that not something you want to try?"

Sebastien reeled back. "Of course I want that."

Something loosened in Nathan. He hadn't realised he needed those words. The idea that Seb wouldn't even want to try must have taken root somewhere deep inside, where he'd been unaware of it until that moment.

"I'm just worried we won't...that we won't be able to do it. Long distance is hard, Nate. We weren't even good at it as friends."

"What do you mean? Of course we were."

Sebastien rolled his eyes. "I didn't even know you were questioning, much less that you'd already realised you were queer. And I never talked to you about what I was going through with having to keep my relationship secret. And I still don't know what the deal is with you and Ang."

"Okay, so we didn't talk about everything, but, Sebastien, I think you're leaving out some pretty big things there. You've always been my best friend. Hell, when my running career was ending, you were the only person in my life who gave me the space to grieve it, and that meant more than anything."

"Really?"

"Glasgow's not nearly as far as the US, and we know what we need to watch out for now. If we're slipping, if we aren't communicating enough, we can keep each other in check."

Sebastien leaned against Nathan, looking up at him, his green eyes wide as Nathan wrapped his arms around him.

"I'm never giving you up now, you know? You're stuck with me," Nathan said quietly.

Sebastien grinned, but it faded quickly. "This is so embarrassing. Nothing we do today will change your mind about leaving, will it?"

Nathan didn't think he'd ever felt so much guilt in his life, but he couldn't stay. He knew deep in his bones that he needed to prove he could do this, could make it on his own without his parents paying his way. That he wasn't just another washed-up has-been who peaked in college. "It's not embarrassing. I love this, I love being out here with you and seeing all the things that make our city special to you, but Sebastien, none of this will change the fact that I have to take this job. This is something I have to do. I have to at least try."

Sebastien nodded, though his smile was dimmer than usual. "I have tickets to the planetarium show at the observatory next. Would you like to go still?"

"Do I want to watch the stars with my boyfriend in the middle of London?" Nathan asked. "Hell yes. Lead the way, baby."

Certain that the discussion wasn't so much resolved as put aside so they could enjoy the rest of the day together, Nathan helped Seb pack up the remains of their picnic and walked with his arm wrapped around him to the observatory. He was sure the show was interesting as astronomers pointed out phenomena in the night sky, but all Nathan would be able to recall if asked was that he had Sebastien in his arms as he stared up at the swirling stars.

It was romantic as fuck, actually. Maybe Sebastien had been on to something with planning this day to convince him to stay, because in that moment, there was nothing he wouldn't do to keep them right there, wrapped up in each other beneath the projected starry sky.

·♥·♥·♥·♥·♥·

Nathan thought the entire date had been next-level romance, but nothing had prepared him for what awaited him when he entered the suite Sebastien had booked for them. For the last few weeks, though they'd tried their best to get time to themselves and certainly enjoyed their stolen moments, but it had been damn difficult between their families, Seb's job, and Mabel—no matter how much he loved her, he was immensely grateful that like many ex-racing dogs, she hadn't quite figured out stairs yet.

The room was large, with a balcony overlooking the Thames off the bedroom and an enormous bathroom with a freestanding glass-sided tub as its centrepiece. A bottle of champagne was chilling in an ice bucket next to the bed.

"Pour us some while I get this all squared away." Sebastien gestured to the bags they'd dumped in a heap at the door as they raced in to explore the room.

"Yes, sir," Nathan said—joking, mostly, but he didn't miss the heat in Sebastien's eyes. It made him wonder if he would want to explore that further. He'd never considered himself particularly kinky, but the idea of Seb taking control was one Nathan's cock, at least, was fully on board with.

Nathan carried the flutes of champagne out to the balcony and set them down. He rested his arms on the balustrade as he looked out over the city. His city. Every landmark, every corner held a different memory. Good and bad, they were imprinted on his soul. Yet, if it weren't for Sebastien, he'd have no qualms at all about leaving again.

He'd always craved independence in a way he'd never quite been able to achieve. His whole life, it had felt like someone else was steering the ship. First his parents, then his coaches. Even his sister, despite being younger, had pushed him, pushed him so hard she'd eventually pushed him away completely.

As he stared out over London, almost absentmindedly cataloguing his past in every piece of the view, Sebastien joined him. He wrapped his arms around Nathan, passing him one of the flutes and clinking it with his own before taking a long sip. Nathan joined his silent toast, the bubbles dancing on his tongue as Seb's mouth found the side of his neck, leaving sloppy open-mouthed kisses down the column of his throat.

"Wanted to romance you so hard, baby," Sebastien groaned. Nathan felt his bulge rub against his backside as he continued his assault, moving down to his shoulder. "So hard you'd never even think of leaving me."

"I'll never leave you, Seb." Nathan groaned. "Not really."

"Want to tie you to my bed and never let you go," Sebastien whispered, flicking his tongue over the shell of Nathan's ear as he pressed up against him. Nathan's own rapidly swelling cock rubbed against his jeans, pressing against the concrete of the balustrade, and he let out a groan that vibrated through his body.

"Wanted to take it so slow, feed you champagne and strawberries before I take you apart on that gorgeous bed." He was tugging at Nathan's jeans now, his nimble fingers popping the button and taking hold of his cock as he whispered, "But I can't resist. Need to feel you now, baby. Want to bend you over and take you right here on the balcony while you look out at the city you're leaving behind."

Nathan choked back a moan as Sebastien pushed his jeans down around his ankles.

"Millions of people out there," Sebastien whispered. "Do you think any of them can see you, can tell how hard you are for me?"

Seb took the champagne flute out of Nathan's hand just in time. He was so keyed up that there wasn't a chance he'd be able to keep hold of it, and dropping it however many stories to the ground below wasn't exactly the conclusion he was hoping this was heading for.

"Arch your back, Nate."

"Yes. Yes, sir," Nate replied, the honorific slipping out involuntarily. It wasn't even a little bit of a joke anymore. Nathan was so filled with want, he'd have done anything Sebastien asked in that moment. He pillowed his head on his arms, arching his back to present himself to Sebastien.

"Beautiful, baby." Seb sighed as he ran a hand over the fleshy globes. Nathan heard him take another swig of champagne, or at least he thought he did, and then Sebastien was pulling his cheeks apart, his tongue laving Nathan's hole sloppily, like he was starving for it. He was sure the city was loud beneath them, but the only sounds he could hear were his own moans and the lapping of Seb's tongue as it speared in and out of him before being swiftly replaced by fingers coated in lube he hadn't even noticed Seb bring outside. It didn't matter though; he was so far gone that the only thing he could focus on was getting Seb's cock in him as soon as bloody possible.

When he finally did, Nathan breathed out a sigh of relief. The entire world seemed to pause for a moment as Sebastien bottomed out inside him, one hand sliding up under his shirt as the other gripped his cock firmly. Then he started to move. It was hard and fast, brutal almost, in a way that Sebastien rarely let himself be, and Nate fucking lived for it. He pushed back as his balls drew up, trying to meet Sebastien thrust for thrust, trusting that the sturdy concrete balustrade could take the weight of them.

The sun started to set, painting the sky in pinks and oranges, but Nathan was seeing stars. He felt Sebastien lose control, his hips stuttering as he spilled inside Nathan, and he was almost there. Almost...

Seb gripped the base of his cock hard, preventing Nathan's impending orgasm from taking over. He let out a strangled sob.

"This is mine," Sebastien groaned. He turned Nathan around and dropped to his knees, sucking his length into his mouth as his fingers replaced his softening cock inside him. He swirled his tongue around the tip before sucking him down his throat and crooking his fingers just so, and Nathan's orgasm came on so fast he couldn't have warned Seb even if he wanted to. But he took his whole load, swallowing it down and then licking him clean.

Spent, Nathan slid down to the balcony floor next to Sebastien, hidden now from the view of the surrounding skyscrapers and whatever their residents may have witnessed. He was sticky with sweat and cum leaked slowly down his thighs but he didn't want to move. They shared a slow kiss, full of tongue and teeth, lips meeting in promise. Nathan could taste himself on Sebastien's tongue, and his cock gave a valiant twitch as they kissed.

Somehow, they did eventually make their way inside. Room service came, but Nathan barely registered accepting it, focused as he was on Sebastien drawing a bath. They made use of the glass tub that literally screamed sex, filling it with bubbles and topping up their champagne. Their food went cold, ignored on its tray as they lounged together in the bubbly water. A sort of dreamy silence fell between them as they sat, feeding each other strawberries and sipping champagne like they were in a film scene.

"Was that okay for you?" Sebastien asked eventually as the water cooled. "I wasn't too... I didn't push, right?"

Nathan pulled his boyfriend into his lap, the move sending water spilling over the sides of the bath. "It was fucking brilliant, baby. I love it when you take control like that. I've loved everything about today. I..." God he was going to say it, wasn't he? It didn't count as a post-coital confession if he'd left a bit of time to settle, right? Because there was no way Nathan was going to be able to stop what was coming next. "I love you, Sebastien."

Sebastien let his head loll back onto Nathan's shoulder and kissed the side of his jaw. "I love you too, Nathaniel," he whispered. Then, softly—so softly, Nathan almost didn't catch it: "Please don't leave me."

There was nothing he could say to that, so he didn't. He bent his neck to capture Sebastien's mouth in a kiss. The kissing quickly turned heated and desperate as they clawed at each other, trying to sink into each other's skin, to leave marks that would last for the time they were apart. The water sloshed out of the bath onto the black tile floor as Sebastien prepped himself, then sank onto Nathan's cock, riding him slowly at first as he clawed at Nathan's chest. Nathan groaned as Seb tweaked his nipples. He snapped his hips to meet Seb's, and they devolved into a frantic, needy race to the finish, the water around them breaking into white-capped waves as they crashed together.

The next morning, Nathan woke up in Sebastien's arms, filled with the cold knowledge that their last night together was over. Once they checked out, he'd only have a few more hours in London before he had to catch the train to whatever lay ahead for him in Scotland, and no matter how much he knew he needed to. He really didn't want to go.

They enjoyed a round of slow, soft sex, taking one last chance to touch every part of each other before they were separated for weeks. They clung to each other through breakfast, packing up their bags and the journey back home where they parted at Nathan's front door with a kiss that felt far too much like a goodbye.

Nathan gathered his things and left for the station but his heart stayed with Seb. He had to give this job his all, but he knew he'd be spending all his free time searching for something in London, something back home where he belonged.

Chapter 9
Sebastien

1 WEEK TO THE SCOTLAND 100

Long distance was bullshit.

Sebastien hated it with every fibre of his being.

Sure, things were good between him and Nathan. But even after their, dare he say it, *epic* date, Nathan had still had to leave. He'd known obviously that one day couldn't change his plans, that Nathan needed this—to strike out on his own and find some sort of validation that he could do things for himself. It still hurt, though. Seb had given him everything, shown Nathan every part of him, even the things no one had ever managed to drag out of him.

A frisson of heat ran through him at the thought.

And still, Nathan had left.

Of course, they spoke every day. Endless texts and video calls, of both the casual and X-rated varieties, were a nightly event. But Sebastien was lonely.

He was lonely and he'd already prepared everything for his mum's race. All that was left to do was load up the car and drive to Scotland, where Nathan was, and yet he didn't even know if he'd manage to see his boyfriend. The race was remote, nowhere near Glasgow, and Nathan was so busy he might not even be able to get the time off to meet up or crew the race with him as they'd promised.

Seb was trying to keep himself busy and not dwell on the disappointment he'd felt when Nate had first told him he may have to work the weekend. For the most part, he'd managed to stay occupied. Darius had reached out to him about the clinic, and they were in the process of having the legal documents drawn up to enter into a partnership to purchase the business. If someone had told him a year ago, or even a couple of months ago, that he'd be starting a business with his ex while pining for his long-distance boyfriend who was Nathaniel Elias Steele, he'd have laughed in their face. Sebastien was doing exactly that, though.

One of the worst things about the impending race was that Sebastien was going to be surrounded by his mum's friends, who had always been far too invested in his love life and were expecting to meet his new boyfriend. It wasn't Nate's fault. It just sucked, was all.

There was a knock at his door. His parents were out for the evening for the first time in ages, and he couldn't help but feel a little bit bitter that they'd chosen now for a night away, when he didn't have anyone he wanted to spend the night with him.

Angie was at the door with Mabel, a frustrated expression on her face as she thrust the lead at Sebastien. "Your child is giving me a damn headache. she hasn't stopped bloody crying at night all week, and I can't sleep. You deal with it."

Sebastien was slightly shell-shocked as he took hold of Mabel's lead. "She's not mine," he half stated, half asked.

"Adopted child then." She shrugged. "Either way, I can't deal, and until Nathan can sort out a place to live that will take dogs, she's your problem."

With that, Angie turned on her heel, leaving Sebastien gaping in the doorway with Mabel's lead still in his outstretched hand. He hadn't even noticed the dog bed full of supplies Ang must have dumped at his feet, but as Mabel looked up at him with her big shiny eyes, Sebastien just sighed.

"You're lucky I love you almost as much as I love your daddy," he whispered to her as he hauled everything inside. Mabel immediately ignored her plush dog bed to flop across the sofa in the front room, leaving only the tiniest corner for Sebastien. Once he settled in, she shuffled around to rest her head in his lap, and he scratched her chin as he chatted.

"I miss him, you know," he mumbled to her. "More than I thought I would, and I already thought I'd miss him a lot."

Sebastien sighed. If he'd resorted to talking out his feelings with Nathan's dog, maybe he should just call his boyfriend so they could at least be lonely together. He shifted slightly to get his phone out of his pocket, earning a whine from Mabel in the process. He shot Nathan a quick text asking if he had time for a call. Then he waited.

And waited.

He watched as the two little ticks turned blue. And still no response came.

Finally, little dots started appearing as Nathan typed a response.

Nathan

2 min

Sebastien sighed, letting his phone drop to his lap as he leaned his head back. It was almost as if their roles had reversed. When they'd first got together, Seb had been burning himself out with long hours at his new job, training, and trying to keep up some semblance of a social life, while Nathan had been unemployed, injured, and mostly lazing around his parents' house. Now, since his new business with Darius was a sure thing, Sebastien had put in his notice at work and was phoning it in even on the shifts he did pick up. He'd stopped making an effort with the few work friends he had started to make, and most of his old friends were still travelling. It was probably a good thing Ang had dropped Mabel with him, actually. It would give him something to do, taking care of her.

After what felt like an hour lost in his thought spiral, Sebastien's phone started to vibrate. Really, it had only been three minutes, but he still groused at Nathan that he'd been waiting ages when he answered the video call.

"I'm sorry, love. I've been thinking about you all day, and I—is that my dog? Have you kidnapped her?" Nathan asked, interrupting whatever he'd been about to say as Mabel popped her head up to see where his voice was coming from.

Nathan's voice turned saccharine as he cooed at the greyhound. "Did Daddy Sebastien steal you away from the big bad lady? Is he treating you good, sweet girl?"

"Angie dropped her off earlier with all her stuff. Guess Mabs has been missing you just as much as I have, so now we can mope about together."

Nathan gave him a soft, sad smile through the screen. "I'm sorry. I miss you both so much, and I'm still looking for something in London, I promise."

"Well, until you find something, Mabel's mine." Sebastien snuggled into the big dog. He knew he was behaving like a petulant child, but it wasn't fair. He'd only just got Nathan back, first as a friend and then as...everything. Only to have him torn away. And as far as he could tell, he was the only one truly bothered by the current arrangement.

Nate was thriving; Sebastien just knew it. As soon as the job had come up, Seb had known it was perfect, and there hadn't been a question in his mind that Nathan would get it. He blamed Scotland. The whole damn country had a lot to answer for as far as Sebastien was concerned. He had half a mind to march on Holyrood when he travelled up this weekend. If Nathan wasn't going to have time for him, at least he'd make the journey worthwhile.

"I can't believe she just dumped Mabs on you without any notice. Did she seem okay?"

Sebastien shrugged. She'd been her usual prickly self, but he hadn't noticed anything out of the ordinary. "Why? Did something happen?"

Sebastien's friendship with Angie might never get back to what it had once been, but he still cared about her, and he knew that deep down, despite whatever had happened to drive a wedge between the siblings—something Sebastien strongly suspected had to do with him—that Nathan still cared about his sister too.

"She texted me earlier asking if we could talk," Nathan replied.

"Is that bad?"

"Just weird. We don't do that. Haven't in years. Family group chat is the only reason I ever know what's going on with her, really."

Thinking back to how tight Nathan and Angie had been as kids made Sebastien's heart ache for them. How did you lose a relationship like that?

"What happened with you two?"

Nathan ruffled his hair with his left hand and sighed. "It wasn't just one thing. I think there was always a lot of resentment there, but we just let it keep building up until one day it didn't have anywhere else to go and..."

"And what?"

"I don't want you to read too much into this..." Nathan said slowly.

"I knew it. I knew it was my fault; she practically spelled it out for me. I just don't know what I could have done that would have made this...this. You two were so close." He couldn't fully articulate the immense guilt that had been growing in the pit of his stomach since his conversation in the kitchen with Angie weeks ago.

"It wasn't your fault, Seb." He could hear the exasperation in Nathan's voice, but frankly, he should have been used to the spirals his brain sent him on by now.

"You remember that night, my last year of sixth form, when we were supposed to go to a warehouse rave in Tottenham, but bottled it at the last minute? It was about two weeks before you and Ang started dating, and I confirmed my place at Harvard."

Of course he remembered. That night had meant everything to Sebastien. They'd run through the streets of London hand in hand, two dumb kids just a little bit too cautious to run with the cool crowd, but reckless enough to stay out all hours drinking cheap cans of lager and racing each other through the park before collapsing together. It was the night Sebastien had realised he was irrevocably gone for Nathan, and also the night he'd realised they'd never be more than friends. Because as they'd lain there in the dewy grass with the chill of the early morning around them, he'd leaned in, determined to kiss him. And Nathan had promptly sat up and backed away, then avoided him for days.

"I'd thought maybe we had a moment, you know?" Nathan said.

He was blushing, but Sebastien was lost. That night was the one that had sent him running into Angie's arms. She'd asked him out twice by that point, and, well, the third time was the charm. Two weeks later, he'd been sure he'd made the right decision when Nate announced he was leaving London to spend four years in America.

Nathan was still talking, explaining that he'd almost kissed Sebastien that night, but that didn't sound right.

Nathan continued, he told Seb about how he'd pulled back, wanting to do things right, not just drunkenly kiss him and laugh it off the next day. Saying he'd got home determined to confess his feelings to Seb, but that he'd found Angie waiting for him there with a knowing look and a litany of reasons why he couldn't be gay and a professional athlete, why he'd be ruining both their careers before they even started if he went for it.

Sebastien sucked in a breath. "She really said that?"

It was a fucking low blow. Though they hadn't dated long, one of the best things about his relationship with Angie had been how supportive she was of his athletics career. Hearing this made it seem like that had all just been a ploy to keep him away from Nathan.

"You know she was wrong, right?"

Nathan looked down. "I know that now, but I was seventeen. I was already so confused by my feelings that it...it made sense. Turns out I couldn't be a professional athlete anyway, so that was a moot point." He laughed sardonically. "But less than three weeks later, you two were a couple, and I felt like I'd been played. I confronted her about it, it got ugly, and then I left without ever apologising. And we just let it fester between us for years until it had eroded whatever foundation we'd had."

Sebastien wished he could hold Nathan and reassure him that whatever had happened between him and Ang could be fixed, but he honestly wasn't sure. "Though this is obviously great for my ego," he joked, "I kind of feel like a piece of shit for hurting you like that. And Angie, I thought. That night, I was so sure I'd imagined that moment and you were so distant the next day that when she asked me out again I just thought, 'why the fuck not?'"

Maybe they could have had four more years together if things had gone differently. Maybe Nathan could have gone to Oxford or Cambridge—or, hell, anywhere else in the UK instead—and they could have been a proper couple the whole time. But other than the distance, Sebastien was happy with where they'd ended up. They were different people than they'd been then, but those experiences hadn't created a wedge between them; if anything, they'd given them a stronger foundation to build on.

"Do you think you'll make it to the race?" Sebastien asked, already dreading the answer but also recognising Nathan's need to get the conversation back on familiar, less treacherous territory.

Nathan's expression tightened, though. "I don't know if I'll make it. They're working me hard. Well, with the biggest event on the calendar coming up, everyone's putting in so much overtime... I'll try though, I don't want to let you down. Or Marie."

"You won't be letting us down, Nate. I'm just worried you're working so much. Is it good, though? You're still happy?"

Nathan paused. "It's... Yeah, it's really good. I'm good at it and I enjoy the work. It's nice to still feel, like, connected to sport in some way. I wasn't sure if it would be. But, Sebastien, I'm still looking for something back in London. Because it doesn't matter what I'm doing, I'd trade it all in a second to be there with you."

There was nothing he could say. It was what it was, and Sebastien desperately wanted both of them to be able to get everything they wanted out of life. After his own experience with unfulfilling work, he'd never begrudge Nathan a career he found purpose in. Nathan needed this after the way his athletics career had ended. He deserved this.

As their conversation wound down and Sebastien managed to extricate himself from a softly snoring Mabel, he was overtaken by a strange sort of calm. He would be fine, and he knew Nathan would be too. This separation wasn't forever. He knew deep in his soul that they were meant to be.

Sure, he might end up crewing on his own this weekend. May have to stay in the romantic B & B he'd rented on his own. But Nathan was it for him, and they'd figure it out eventually.

Chapter 10
Nathan

The Scotland 100

It was a four-hour bus ride from Glasgow to Forres where the Scottish 100 was starting. Nathan had put in a ridiculously long night at work to be able to take the weekend off, and he was running so late he was convinced he was going to miss the start altogether.

There was no chance of meeting up with Seb beforehand, and mobile signal was spotty as hell, so he checked in quickly with the race coordinator and then shared a lift with another runner's crew to near the fifth aid station, where he'd agreed to start pacing Marie. Seb was planning to take over from the seventh until the first campsite.

He hadn't expected to be there at all. He'd been telling the truth when he told Sebastien his job was intense and that the overtime was insane. But the call with his sister that he'd put off until the last minute had changed everything, and he'd tried to let Seb know but couldn't get hold of him. He'd finally managed to reach Marie's running group while he was on the bus, so at least she should be expecting him.

Speaking to Angie had been enlightening in a few ways. She'd apologised for being a manipulative, delusional shit at sixteen—her words, not his—and they'd hashed out the other issues that had festered over the years. She saw him as the golden child who got everything he wanted, and felt like she had to work ten times as hard to get any sort of recognition. He admitted he hadn't realised it and she'd made it clear that was the worst part, but Ang had receipts. Of course she did. He felt guilty about it, but not enough to forgive her unnecessary cruelty hidden behind a veneer of being "honest."

Or enough to excuse how she'd obviously tried to use Seb like some sort of prize in the sibling-war Nathan hadn't even realised he'd been part of. He'd called her out on it and for the first time in years had seen something that passed for regret come over his sister's face.

"Have you ever thought you knew exactly what you wanted and realised you had been completely and utterly wrong once you got it?" she'd asked. "Seb was...an idea to me then. Abstract. The hot boy-next-door, perfect first boyfriend material, and you were in the way— just like you were in the way of everything I wanted."

Nathan had nodded. He hadn't known what to say.

"And then I got him, and I knew right away I didn't really have him. You were it for him, all along, and I really just wanted him to be my friend, like we had been as kids. I felt awful about it when Seb came out to me, but you were gone and you never showed any sign of being interested in men, so I figured I hadn't really done anything wrong. You'd never have been anything anyways."

He'd snorted at that. Seb had always been it for him, but that didn't mean he hadn't done his own exploring, he just hadn't told his little sister about it, because why would he have?

"So I'm sorry. I'm sorry for forcing my way in. I'm sorry for seeing you as an obstacle instead of a brother, and I'm sorry Seb got hurt in the process."

Nathan had never imagined he'd actually hear those words leave Ang's mouth.

That wasn't what had changed everything, though. It had been nice to clear the air with his sister, obviously, and maybe one day they'd even be close again, or as close as adult siblings could really be with half a lifetime of resentment to overcome. What had changed things was that she hadn't just been calling to clear the air. She'd called with a proposal.

It turned out Ang had moved home because of a messy breakup—one he hadn't even been aware of, which made him feel like the worst older brother on earth. No matter how he felt about his sister, the idea of some arsehole hurting her didn't sit right. Now, she wanted out of London. She'd booked a round-the-world ticket with her best friend, Noelia, and was leaving to find herself, with Bali as their first stop. Noelia's work had let her take a six-month sabbatical, but they needed a replacement, and Nathan was uniquely qualified as Noelia worked as an event coordinator for a sporting events company whose flagship was the London Marathon.

He hadn't said anything to Seb yet; he hadn't wanted to disappoint him in case nothing came of it, but he had a good feeling. Good enough that he didn't even care that he was relying on his baby sister to fix all his problems. If he'd been less excited about living in the same city as Sebastien, it might have bothered him, made him feel like he wasn't succeeding on his own terms. But fuck that. Sebastien had always been his. Even when he was Angie's, even when he was Darius's, it didn't feel big-headed at all to admit that they'd always belonged to each other.

Nate prepared everything at the aid station just as Marie had requested. A change of socks and shoes, food, electrolytes—all ready to go. The knowing smile he got from Marie when she arrived felt like a promise that everything would work out. She knew, obviously, that he wasn't just here to help out; he was here for something so much bigger. He was here for his future. And his future's name was Sebastien Andrew Murphy.

Nathan ran for longer than he had, possibly in his entire life. Marie was a goddamn machine. His shoulder barely twinged as he pumped his arms, watching their pace and checking she was feeling okay. He knew Seb would be at the handoff, but they wouldn't have much time. Just enough to get Marie refuelled and off again. It would be enough, though. He'd see him after, and if things went to plan, every damn day for the rest of his life.

At the first of the aid stations he was passing through with Marie, he grabbed the water on offer and a cup of sugary tea to keep him going, but he declined the offer of food from the volunteers, not wanting to take any fuel away from the runners covering obscene distances he'd never even consider.

He knew Marie was feeling it. She must have been deep in the pain cave, because she barely spoke as they ran. Nathan was surprisingly grateful; the time and the challenging terrain gave him a chance to think through everything that was going on in his life. Focusing on his plan for the evening, on finding Sebastien to surprise him with his good news and a question, was keeping him going. He could see the next aid station ahead of them now, their handoff point. He turned to Marie with a grin and offered her a high five as she stumbled in, giving her number to the volunteers as Seb rushed over, thrusting electrolytes and food at her and checking her for any strains or injuries. As an ultra-runner, it had to be handy having a medical professional on your crew.

Nathan met Seb's eyes and watched a grin split his face as he fussed over his mother. That right there was the love of his life.

Marie was ready to go, but she paused. "Oh, kiss your damn boyfriend hello, Sebastien," she said. "I'm not going to lose sleep over an extra few seconds."

They kissed for the first time in weeks, surrounded by volunteers and exhausted runners with Seb's mum looking on, proud and impatient. Nathan couldn't have planned it better if he'd tried.

Nathan's next port of call was the runners' checkpoint and campsite for the night. When he arrived, he got busy grabbing Marie's drop bag and making sure everything was ready for her to eat and crash into bed—she'd have an early start the next morning on the next leg of the race. Once everything was ready, he settled in to watch runners arrive in various states of distress. This did not look like fun. He couldn't fathom why anyone would ever take up such an insane sport.

Then, through the crowd of bedraggled runners, he spotted him, his head of mahogany curls thrown back in laughter as he ran alongside his mum. Nathan jumped to his feet and rushed towards Sebastien as they approached, sweeping him into his arms and lifting him with a strength he was surprised he still had in him.

Seb squealed and flailed as Marie and several of the surrounding runners laughed. Nathan barely registered them, though. He only had eyes for the man in his arms.

"I thought you couldn't make it?" Sebastien said when Nathan set him back on the ground.

"It was very last minute." He laughed, burying his face in Sebastien's shoulder and inhaling the scent of him, all sweat and salt and the lingering sweetness of the energy gels he'd probably spilled on his hands mid-race.

"Fuck, I missed you," he nearly sobbed as it hit him, the adrenaline of everything that had happened over the last few days leaving him all at once.

Sebastien took pity on him, wrapping his arms around him as they walked together to get Marie checked in. She waved them off, chattering with her friends as she made her way to the dinner that had been laid out for the runners.

Sebastien led Nate to the nearby car park, then drove them what he assumed was a short distance to a quaint B&B they'd booked together when they'd first started planning for the race and realised, to their great relief, that crew didn't have to camp.

If you'd asked him after, Nathan couldn't, even under threat of severe bodily harm, recount the exact sequence of events that had led to him lying spread-eagled with his face smushed into a hand-stitched pink quilt in a room with the most quintessentially English floral wallpaper he'd ever seen. But Sebastien was a sure weight next to him, whispering sweet things in his ear and tracing slow circles on his back as he came back to himself.

"Have you slept at all, baby?" Seb asked.

Nathan shook his head. "Worked late, bus up, early morning," he said with as much coherence as he could muster.

"Shhh. Get some rest, love," Sebastien whispered.

"No. Want to tell you..." Nathan trailed off as sleep claimed him.

When he woke, the muted colours of the setting sun were streaming into the room. It couldn't have been late, and Sebastien was sat in bed next to him, a book in one hand and the other resting on Nathan's shoulder in a gentle but possessive grip, as though he was making sure he was still there. Sebastien's glasses were perched on the end of his nose, and Nathan took a moment to just admire him before he shifted and whispered, "Hi."

It came out softer and more shyly than he'd intended, but still had the right effect. Seb snapped his book shut and lowered his head to kiss him.

It felt like coming home.

"You're crazy, you know, running a trail marathon on no sleep like that. Mum wouldn't have been upset if you'd skipped it. You could have hurt yourself," Sebastien said. It would have been more effective at calming Nathan's grin if he hadn't used that authoritative tone that always got him going.

"Don't worry." He smirked. "I've got a great physio."

Sebastien rolled his eyes. "You have, but I can't do much from a distance."

Nathan couldn't hold his in excitement anymore. "Good thing I'll be back in London permanently soon, then, isn't it?"

Sebastien blinked at him. Admittedly, it wasn't quite the reaction he'd hoped for.

"Nathan, you can't quit for me—" he started.

"I'm not. I got an offer in London and it's perfect. I swear, I wouldn't put that kind of pressure on you," he explained quickly. "It's the event coordinator job for the marathon."

Sebastien frowned. "Ang's friend works there, doesn't she?"

"Yeah. Angie recommended me, believe it or not. They're off travelling together—some new-age yogi bullshit is calling to her."

Sebastien snorted. "And you're okay with that?"

Now that Sebastien understood the issues between Nathan and his sister, he always treaded lightly when she came up.

"I figure it would be hypocritical of me to talk you into working with your ex and then not even be willing to take a bit of help from my own sister," Nathan replied.

Sebastien laughed. "So you're really coming back?"

"I'm really coming back. But, Seb, I don't think we can be neighbours anymore."

"What? Why not?" Sebastien's face fell.

"Well, 'cause I was really hoping we could both move out. Together."

"You want me to live with you?"

Nathan ran a hand through his hair. "Yeah. I mean...if you'd like that? We won't be able to get much, and we may have to move further out, or maybe east? I don't know, but I'd really love to live with you."

Sebastien was silent for a moment, and Nathan waited with bated breath. "I'd love to live with you, Nate," he murmured. "I love you and I'm never letting you go."

Nathan didn't know who moved first, but suddenly they were kissing and he was touching every part of Sebastien he could get his hands on.

"Fuck, I missed you so much, baby," Sebastien whispered in his ear. "Missed the feel of your skin, your taste, the way you whimper."

Nathan responded by doing just that as Seb peppered kisses down his naked chest.

"I'm going to take you apart nice and slow, baby. Show you that every part of you is mine. And every part of me is yours." Sebastien kissed his injured shoulder, his tongue tracing the freckle patterned there that had emerged in the hot sun of the race. "This shoulder," he whispered. "Mine."

Nathan groaned and his cock twitched as Sebastien left a messy open-mouthed kiss on his shoulder before moving down to his collarbone and repeating the process. "Mine." He stared for a second before continuing down to Nathan's chest, taking possession of every inch of Nathan's body with his tongue and teeth.

The process left Nathan hard and aching. Desperate to be touched. Desperate to be filled. When Sebastien finally reached his cock, he granted Nathan's wish by slicking a single finger with lube and pressing it slowly inside him.

"Now I'm going to fuck you, baby," he whispered. "Is that what you want?"

"Yes, yes, please," Nathan babbled.

"Yes, what?" Sebastien sat back on his heels as he removed his hands from Nathan completely.

Nathan nearly sobbed his "Yes, sir."

Sebastien grinned and kissed him again as he pressed in with two fingers this time. "I'm going to give it to you nice and slow, baby. Make it last. And then, when you're almost there, I want you to tell me and we're going to flip. I want you to fuck me so hard I see fucking stars," he ordered. Because ordered was the only word for it, and Nathan was more than willing to comply. "Can you do that?"

"Yes. Yes, sir."

"Good boy."

Sebastien smirked, knowing exactly what he was doing to Nathan as he pressed a third finger inside him, stretching him just enough before dripping a generous amount of lube over himself and pushing in so fucking slowly Nathan wanted to scream. He kept true to his word, manoeuvring Nathan as he dragged his cock in and out, brushing his prostate and forcing sounds out of Nathan's mouth that he hadn't even realised he was capable of making. He felt like he was being taken apart and rearranged. He felt everything, and then he cried out and grabbed the base of his cock, willing himself not to come, desperate to follow Sebastien's directions to a T.

"You almost there, baby?" Seb asked.

Nathan whimpered. "So fucking close. I don't know if I can wait."

"Yes, you can, baby. You're incredible. You can do this, just hold on and let me ride you."

Nathan tried to respond as Sebastien slid out of him before flipping him over and lining himself up over Nathan's hard, leaking cock. He didn't know when he'd prepped himself, but he must have because he slid down slowly but with no pain in his eyes, only pleasure as he enveloped him.

"I'm not going to last," Nathan choked out.

"You don't need to." Sebastien grinned. Then he was riding him, driving up and down at a rate that probably rivalled the pace he'd set in the race earlier that day, and Nathan was lost. He grabbed for Sebastien's bobbing cock, jerking it sloppily until he felt him convulse above him. That was enough to tip Nathan over the edge, his orgasm exploding out of him just seconds before Seb's cum sprayed out over his chest.

They collapsed together, Nathan's softening cock slipping out of Sebastien, cum spilling onto the sheets. They probably needed to clean up, shower, and go get dinner or something; they did have a lot more running to do tomorrow. But it could wait. All of it could wait. Because he had Sebastien in his arms. He was Nathan's, and Nathan was his, and they had the rest of their lives ahead of them.

The perfect place for them both to land, softly, safely. Forever.

Chapter 11
Epilogue

2 YEARS LATER

"End of an era." Nathan sighed as he locked the door of the flat they'd rented for the past two years behind them.

"Beginning of an even better one, though." Sebastien laughed as he plucked the keys out of his hands and sealed them in an envelope to drop with the letting agency. They'd been planning this move for nearly a year, and it almost felt surreal that the day was finally here. The day they would move into their own home, one they'd own together, both of their names on the title.

The location was perfect—further out than where they'd grown up, but Walthamstow was still close enough that it was a reasonable tube journey for both of them to get to work. Besides, Seb's job rarely took him into the clinic anymore. Most pro athletes wanted treatment in their own homes or gyms, and the charity programme he was offering now had him travelling all over.

He was thrilled about the house, but it was awkward timing in some ways because Nathan was meant to be up in Scotland in just two days. Not for work, thankfully. Seb really would chain him to their bed, and not in the fun way, if he ever even hinted at doing the long-distance thing again. No, this time Nathan was running a fifty miler alongside Sebastien's mum. It wasn't his first ultra by any means—he'd well and truly caught the bug for it.

What Nathan didn't know was that Seb had big plans this time. He'd arranged a great crew and cheering squad for Nathan and made sure his family would be at the finish line. It was going to be perfect. But first, they had a house to move into.

·♥·♥·♥·♥·♥·

Despite working for the London Marathon for the past two years, Nathan had never actually run in the event. He'd never done marathon distance at all, actually. It was Sebastien's best distance, and when your boyfriend was about as close to elite marathon times as one could get without being an actual professional, well...Nathan was competitive, okay? He needed a different event.

Sebastien didn't run London now either, though. The first year of coordinating, Nathan had panicked when the woman manning the elite tent had come down with food poisoning last minute and had roped Seb into helping out. He knew most of the athletes anyway, and it was good publicity for his business.

Instead of marathons, Nathan had jumped feet first into ultras. He'd known he was hooked that first time pacing Sebastien's mum in Scotland, though he'd never have admitted it then. He hadn't done his first one until a year ago, but now it was like an addiction.

This race was brutal, though. He wasn't as prepared as he wanted to be—sorting out the move last minute had meant he hadn't rested properly before the race, and travelling up with Seb, staying in the same place they had when they first got together...well, he hadn't had a lot of sleep last night. Still, it was nearly finished, less than a single marathon left to go, and he'd had a delicious peanut butter and jam tortilla wrap and some flat coke at the last aid station that had reinvigorated him.

He wasn't a great ultra-runner, firmly mid-pack, but nobody cared about times out here; it was all about finishing the race. It took just as much grit and determination to come last as it did to come first.

He kept going, thundering down the rocky path, focusing on keeping his landings soft on the ground beneath him.

Three hours later, with the finish line in view and only a couple of other runners beside him, Nathan slowed to look at the scenery. He never would have done this when he first started, too competitive, but now he liked to take in the atmosphere.

The crowd at the finish was unusually large today, and as he approached, he realised he recognised almost every face among them. He let the other two runners get a decent lead on him, realising that something was going on. Reg, a runner his age who he'd done a few events with, shot him a questioning look as he ran past. Nathan nodded towards the group and laughed. "Don't want to steal anyone's thunder."

"Ooh er, someone's got a fan club," Reggie said with a smile, high-fiving Nathan as he gave the race the finishing kick it probably deserved.

Nathan saw one particular grinning face as he approached. He crossed the line and accepted his medal, moving forwards out of the way in case there was anyone finishing behind him that he hadn't spotted, then nearly collapsed into Seb's waiting arms. Sebastien broke the embrace quickly, and Nathan threw his arms out to keep his balance, confused for a moment by the scene before him as Sebastien went down on one knee and started to speak.

"Nathaniel Elias Steele," he said, "I know it's not a belt buckle, but I was wondering if you'd be into adding another piece of bling to your collection, permanently?"

Nathan snorted, and Sebastien's expression turned earnest. "Nathan, I've loved you since before I knew what the word meant. Would you do me the honour of becoming my husband?"

There was nothing else to say but yes.

A Note from Kim

Thank you for reading *Soft Landings.*

If you enjoyed the novella I would be honoured if you'd consider leaving a review. Reviews really do make a huge difference for indie authors like me!

·♥·♥·♥·♥·♥·

This wasn't planned to be my first release! The idea for it came from a scene in *Your Pace or Mine* between Darius and Seb that made me feel like Sebastien really deserved to have his story told.

It was so much fun to write Seb and Nathan's story. The idea of athletes at the end of their careers, or whose careers never quite take off has always been so interesting to me and was something I wanted to explore in this prequel.

This is the prequel to my debut novel *Your Pace or Mine*, which is set four years after the main events of *Soft Landings*. The *Running for the Romance* series as a whole centres around queer runners finding their happily ever afters, and I hope you'll continue to join me on the journey.

If you'd like to keep up with developments in the series, you can sign up for my newsletter on kimstephensonauthor.com

Acknowledgements

I wrote the majority of this book while staying with my in-laws, so thank you to them for their support, even though they may never read this book... unless it gets translated that is!

My Mum, always my biggest supporter. My partner and son because you are just the best, even if you get annoyed when I talk too much about writing.

The amazing friends that have supported me along the way. A particular shout-out to Kelly for the alpha read and extensive conversation about character names.

My editing team, beta readers and cover designers—thank you for your support in bringing Seb and Nate's story to life.

To you, my readers, thank you from the bottom of my heart!

Additional titles by Kim Stephenson

Your Pace or Mine, a novel by Kim Stephenson

True love is a marathon, not a sprint

Elite marathoner Darius Hewitt is the golden boy of British athletics until a media scandal brings his Olympic dreams crashing down. With his reputation in tatters, Darius reluctantly agrees to help out at a charity running clinic, hoping to regain favour with the Olympic selection committee.

Enter Jamie, a sharp-witted West End dancer, training for his first marathon. Jamie comes with a crumbling career of his own, outrageous fundraising target, and a whole different brand of publicity challenges.

In the lead up to the London Marathon, a fake relationship seems like the perfect solution for both their image problems, so Darius and Jamie strike a deal.

But the more time they spend together, the less pretend it starts to feel.

Can they stop running from their fears long enough to give love a shot?

Your Pace or Mine is a contemporary MM sports romance packed with fake dating, sharp banter, spice and plenty of running.

Coming September 2025

·♥·♥·♥·♥·♥·

Stride for Stride by Kim Stephenson

Rivals on the road. Teammates on paper. But could there be more to the story?

Jackson and Elliott have been neck-and-neck since their first race—two elite marathoners constantly pushing each other to the limit. But with the Olympics looming, they're forced to do the unthinkable: train *together*.

Altitude camp means long runs, cold nights, and the kind of tension that's not just competitive anymore. When a single moment shatters the fragile line between rivals and something much more complicated, both men are left breathless, for reasons that have nothing to do with their last tempo run.

But between their very different upbringings, and the pressure of the Olympics, their chance at love might not make it to the finish line.

Can they go stride for stride towards something real, or will the world pull them apart before they've even begun?

Stride for Stride is a the sizzling follow up to *Your Pace or Mine*. It is a standalone MM Rivals-to-Lovers Sports Romance and book two in the *Running for the Romance* series.

Coming in 2026

Sign up for updates on kimstephensonauthor.com

Running Glossary

- **5K:** A 5-kilometre race (3.107 miles)
- **10K:** A 10-kilometer race (6.2 miles)
- **Aid Station:** A designated area during races where runners can get water, sports drinks, medical aid, and other supplies
- **Altitude Camp:** A training camp located at high elevation to improve endurance by enhancing oxygen utilisation, common practice for endurance athletes
- **Ballot:** A lottery system used to allocate limited race spots to applicants, common in major marathons
- **Bonking:** Sudden fatigue and energy loss due to depleted glycogen stores during endurance activities
- **BQ (Boston Qualifier):** A marathon finish time that qualifies a runner for the Boston Marathon, the standard is updated annually
- **Bun Huggers**: A style of technical athletic shorts designed for women. Also known as 'briefs' or 'competition briefs'

- **Cadence:** The number of steps a runner takes per minute
- **Charity Bib:** A race entry given in exchange for a fundraising commitment to a charity, especially common in over-subscribed or balloted events
- **Chip Time:** The actual time it takes a runner to finish a race, starting when they cross the starting line, measured by a tracking chip on their number or shoe
- **Corral:** A designated area where runners are grouped by pace before the race begins
- **DFL (Dead Freakin' Last):** Slang for finishing last in a race
- **DNF (Did Not Finish)** A runner who starts but does not complete a race.
- **DNS (Did Not Start):** A runner who was registered but did not start the race
- **DOMS (Delayed Onset Muscle Soreness):** Muscle pain and stiffness that sets in 24–72 hours after intense exercise
- **Distance Runner:** An athlete who specialises in longer races, typically 5K and above
- **Drafting:** Running closely behind another runner to reduce air resistance
- **Dreadmill:** A more honest term for the treadmill, an indoor running machine that allows you to run in place

- **Dynamic Stretching:** Active movements that stretch muscles to prepare the body for running (as opposed to static stretching)

- **Elite:** A top-level competitive runner, often sponsored and invited to races with special perks and prize money

- **Fartlek:** A Swedish term meaning "speed play"; unstructured speed intervals during a run

- **Finishing Kick:** A runner's final burst of speed at the end of a race

- **Foam Roller:** A cylindrical tool used to massage and relieve tight muscles

- **Form:** A runner's posture and body mechanics while running

- **Front Runner:** A runner who leads a race from the start, often setting the pace

- **Gels:** Concentrated carbohydrate packets used during long runs or races for energy, they come in a wide range of flavours

- **Glycogen:** The stored form of glucose in muscles and liver, used as energy during exercise

- **Gun Time:** The official race time based on the starting gun, not individual chip start

- **Half Marathon:** A 13.1-mile (21.1 km) race

- **Heel-striking:** Running form where the heel contacts the ground first, sometimes associated with inefficient running
- **Hill Sprints:** Short, high-intensity running uphill to build strength and power
- **Hitting the Wall:** A dramatic energy crash during long runs when glycogen is depleted, in a marathon often occurs between miles 18 and 22
- **Intervals:** Specific timed efforts followed by rest periods; key part of speed training
- **ITB Syndrome(Iliotibial Band Syndrome):** A common running injury causing outer knee pain from overuse
- **Jeffing:** A run-walk method developed by Jeff Galloway, using planned walk breaks to conserve energy and reduce injury risk
- **Lactate Threshold:** The exercise intensity at which lactate begins to accumulate rapidly in the blood, often used to guide tempo run pace
- **Marathon:** A26.2-mile (42.195 km) race
- **Negative Split:** Running the second half of a race faster than the first half
- **Over-striding:** Taking steps that extend too far in front of the body, which can lead to inefficiency or injury
- **Overtraining:** Excessive training without adequate rest,

leading to fatigue, poor performance, or injury

- **Pace:** The speed at which a runner is moving, typically measured in minutes per mile or kilometre
- **PB (Personal Best):** A runner's fastest time for a given distance within any context, including informal runs or training sessions
- **PR (Personal Record):** A runner's fastest time for a race in an official, timed event
- **Recovery Run:** A slow, easy run done to help muscles recover between hard workouts
- **Runner's High:** A euphoric feeling experienced during or after running, often linked to endorphins
- **Soft Landing:** A gentle foot strike that minimises impact forces during running, often encouraged for injury prevention
- **Speedwork:** A general term for workouts designed to improve speed, such as intervals or tempo runs
- **Splits:** The time it takes to complete each segment of a race, such as every mile or kilometre
- **Sprinter:** An athlete who specialises in short-distance, high-speed races (typically 100m to 400m)
- **Strides:** Short bursts of controlled, fast running to improve form and leg turnover

- **Taper:** A reduction in training volume leading up to a race to allow for full recovery
- **Tempo Run:** A sustained effort run at a "comfortably hard" pace, near lactate threshold
- **Ultra Marathon:** Any race longer than the marathon distance, typically starting at 50 km (31 miles) and up
- **VO2 Max:** The maximum amount of oxygen the body can utilise during intense exercise
- **Zone 2 Pace:** A low-intensity running pace that builds aerobic endurance; typically 60–70% of max heart rate
- **Zone 5 Pace:** A high-intensity pace used for short intervals; around 90–100% of max heart rate
- **Zone 6 Pace:** Maximum effort sprint pace, often unsustainable for more than a few seconds

About the author

Kim Stephenson crafts heartfelt queer sports romances, celebrating love, identity, and perseverance. Through writing, Kim shares a passion for characters embracing their true selves, one step at a time.

Kim currently lives in the U.K. and when not writing, can often be found lacing up a pair of trainers to hit the local pavements or trails.

Printed in Dunstable, United Kingdom

68011285R00067